George Hopkins

Ralph's Possession

A simple record of how it was given him and what he did with it

George Hopkins

Ralph's Possession
A simple record of how it was given him and what he did with it

ISBN/EAN: 9783337084875

Printed in Europe, USA, Canada, Australia, Japan

Cover: Foto ©Andreas Hilbeck / pixelio.de

More available books at **www.hansebooks.com**

RALPH'S POSSESSION.

*A Simple Record of How It was Given Him and
What He Did With It.*

By George Hopkins.

Ah, were it possible to show
How sweet Thy love may be!
With Thee, however, tears may flow,
In every joy with Thee.
From the Latin.

Unto you, therefore, who believe, He is precious.
Epistle of Peter.

BOSTON
D LOTHROP COMPANY

Entered, according to Act of Congress, in the year 1873,

By D. LOTHROP & CO.,

In the Office of the Librarian of Congress, at Washington.

CONTENTS.

RALPH'S POSSESSION.

—

CHAPTER I.

RALPH CUSHING.

CRASH! Plunge! Halt!

That was all. There was nothing deadly, nothing fearful.

Only a sudden, brief episode; an astonishment; an arrest. The fine carriage that had been rolling on so well refused to go, and refused explanation. Its two splendid horses, exactly alike, and totally different, stood still;

but quiet, handsome William Penn stood properly surprised, on all-fours; while the high-mettled Philip stood very erect on his hindermost parts. But Philip was soon controlled by the young driver, and shamed, perhaps, by Penn's dignity.

The two occupants of the carriage, mother and son, were in resemblance and contrast as the two horses. Looking not unlike (the less so that the son was rather old of his age, and the mother was well-preserved), — the mother, seeing all safe, was in no perturbation whatever; while the son, in all self-possession, was duly excited to make out the dilemma. Having controlled Philip, he fell into antics himself; for an adventure always put gay Ralph Cushing into extra spirits. However, here was his mother to be taken care of; and his good heart and head, alike, sobered with the emergency.

    .   .   .   .   .

" The axletree forward, is quite broken! Now what is to be done? The town is only two miles distant. You cannot walk that, my poor mamma ; but *I* might."

"My dear son !" Then, checking herself, the lady added, "Ah, well! you have some good plan. If it were but daylight!"

"Never mind, mamma, we will make the most of the moonlight. It may answer our need quite as well."

"Yes. And how soft! how perfect! It was at full moon when we left your father five weeks ago. Poor papa!" The voice trembled, and the quick sigh came.

"Now, mother mine, let us talk about the present predicament." There was a slight, a very slight sharpness in the voice, — just a hint of impatience. But there was no impatience in the gesture with which he stroked her chastened face, as he drew it toward his own and kissed it.

"And *what* a predicament!" he continued more gayly. "We *are* in a predicament, sure enough ; but Ralph Cushing is not the man to stay *here* long. Wouldn't you feel safe on my broad shoulders ? "

"Safe, but not comfortable," replied Mrs. Cushing, with a quiet humor not inconsistent with her gentle nature.

"But do you feel comfortable now, and where you are?"

"Comfortable, but not safe. I could pass the night in the carriage very well, but I prefer to be elsewhere."

"How singular!" said Ralph. "Not safe in in a place so lonely that there is no finding anybody in it, and no getting out of it! However, it would not be chivalric in me to leave you here, nor inventive in me to avoid leaving you by staying myself. What do you think of better than my shoulders?"

"I think you are taking it coolly, Ralph my boy. But you must have your pleasant thoughts always. Oh! my happy unhappy boy!"

'Now, mother, don't make yourself unhappy about your happy boy. *Cool?* Oh! the American *sang froid* is worth everything. Imagine a Frenchman, now, in this case. The whole affair would be wisely dissected, and nothing done. But you see I, being an American, work while I talk. Here are the horses already unhitched, — 'detached,' Professor Payne would say, — and at your service; or *one* of them is at your service. Penn is the safest; and we'll soon have his harness off, and saddle him somehow."

"What a pity it is that we had to leave Zed yesterday!" said Mrs. Cushing, "it is so hard for you to do all this, besides driving me all these two evenings! I hope the poor fellow is better."

"Oh, it is not hard; it is easy," said the young man blithely. "That is, easy when done for you, mamma, I mean."

"Ralph, you are making yourself finer with every sentence."

"Thank you, my mother," said Ralph, putting down his face meekly; "Now your steed is ready; or, rather, he is ready to be ready; but what for a saddle? Can you spare a shawl?"

"Why yes, — such a night as this, — too

lovely to allow of counting any inconvenience a hardship. Dear Ralph, how shall I hold on? with a shawl for a saddle! You know I am not practiced in riding these many years. And now, neither stirrup nor pommel! My courage forsakes me."

But your faith does not, mother. You do not doubt I will hold you on. Now that is the assurance of faith, is it not?"

"Ralph, my dear son, the expressions of God's word are too precious for any light citation."

"I wounded you, mother mine! Ah, well! I thought you were fond of illustrations."

"Yes, but without lightness if the Word of God is touched."

"Mamma, why did you say 'precious?' why not *sacred*, or something with an ecclesiastical tone?"

"Indeed," said his mother, "I don't know why. I did not weigh the words."

Ralph thought he knew, but there was no time to say so. He had during this conversation improvised a seat, if not exactly *saddle*, that suited the emergency excellently. Two large shawls, each made into a compact roll, and so strapped together as to allow a sufficient space between them, were placed one on each side of Penn's ample back. Between them a cloak thickly folded, and the whole was secured by a little contriving with girth-straps.

"Penn, you look well, good fellow," said the young man, quite satisfied with his achievements. "Now mamma, you will sink so well into the cloak that you can't well fall off—or fall *out*, I may say. In the first place, I put you on a secure foundation. In the next place, I hold you on—" He checked himself suddenly, and then as quickly added; "mamma, I am not 'light.' But *you* are, little mother," he said, taking her tenderly out of the carriage and placing her softly down between the shawls— "light as a feather, I don't believe Penn knows you are on his back. Now how will it go? do you feel ' safe, but not comfortable '?"

"Quite comfortable, thanks, my dear Ralph. You have made quite a success with your contrivance."

The valises and travelling bags were hung across Philip's royal back. Penn was tractable enough to the guidance of his rider ; leaving Ralph free to lead Philip, with a hand for his mother if needed.

"Are you quite warm with only your light shawl?" he asked.

"Oh, quite warm, my dear son. These Tennessee woods are so sweet; and this is one of the richest sections we have met. To think of that two-mile walk for you; — why Ralph, what are you turning the corners for ? "

"To make a short cut."

"You puzzle me. Please explain."

"Well mamma, half a mile is quicker done than two miles. If you are not soon sheltered I fear you will be quite sick. That pretty white farm-house — or call it by some other name — that we passed a half-mile back, I am sure is hospitably disposed, and has a spare room for you beside."

"Indeed, I did not know we had passed such a house," said Mrs. Cushing.

"No," said Ralph "you were enjoying a nap and I was enjoying the moon-rising. For once you were in dreams while I was taking in realities, my good, practical mamma. I was studying the pretty homestead, and am satisfied that there is a spare room in front, on the west side."

"Ralph! Ah, no! but the longer way is a long walk for you; really, on every other account I would rather go on to Cousin Cecilia's. We don't know what kind of people they are at this house you speak of. Besides, asking so much at the hands of strangers should be avoided if possible."

"I don't deny you speak wisely," said Ralph; "you never speak otherwise. But I fear for your strength. And then, these southern people are so free and cordial, — or, if not cordial, magnificent in good manners, socially; let them alone politically. But we are wasting time. I have a strange drawing toward the strange, pretty house; but am quite equal to the long walk."

"Then, Ralph dear, I decide to go on to Mariondale. No doubt Southern hospitality is munificent; but I would rather not disturb those good people at this late hour, and with no plea whatever but my own convenience."

The horses were turned again. The son walked by the mother, leading Philip, and looking manly enough to lead an army. The clear Southern moonlight lent a wonderful expression to his marked features, as well as to the rich, woody landscape that lay out before and on either hand, in almost supernatural festoonery beneath the silver stream. Both parties fell into silence. The horses were good walkers; and the mere matter of progression, as things were, kept all well occupied. Mrs. Cushing spoke first, —

"What an unspeakably droll ending of our journey, Ralph. You are taking a more tremendous view of it, I dare say."

And, to tell the truth, Ralph was wonderfully sensitive about arriving at Cousin Cecilia's in that fashion; and his gay temperament, always alive to the ludicrous, had been unwontedly sobered by the responsibility of the moment. He was happily aroused by his mother's remark, and for a few minutes the air was ringing with his speeches and his merriment. But this soon passed; and when a silence advertised his mother that his thinking brain was really in more quiet mood, she said : —

" Ralph, it seems to me that we cannot divide the social from the political; at least not in our country."

Ralph looked up an instant inquisitively; puzzled at the abrupt remark, and then said, "Oh! you have that criticism for my expression as to social manners hereabouts. I think I was using the word social in the limited sense

that attaches to the home life and neighborly in-
tercourse. *Domestic Etiquette*, if you please;
but something more than that. The cultivation
of, and appeal to, the feelings, as well as the regard for what is correct in expression. In this aspect, it strikes me, that social manners are more
identified with the religious than with the political. That is, religious life, more than political
life, affects the home circle."

"Yes, I think you are right," said his mother.

"But you would not say that there is more
religious life in the homes of the South than in
those of the North?"

"Perhaps not, — no; I mean just this: that
wherever high-toned living exists, the entrance
of true religious belief tends to perfect what
were otherwise defective. Refined manners are
not always considerate or gentle. Nothing so
completes the gentleman in the way of refinement, as a heart responsive to the grace and
truth of Christ. You know I am not speaking
out of experience; but I think I have seen
this."

"Yes, you are right again," said his mother, looking at him fondly, somewhat wonderingly, and with unwonted yearning. He did not notice this, but fell again into revery; only asking now and then if she was getting too weary, or was keeping warm; and once playfully manifesting great anxiety to know whether she felt the more safe, or the more comfortable.

2

CHAPTER II.

RALPH AND HIS FATHER.

THE scene recorded in the preceding pages has seemed to introduce Ralph Cushing and his mother somewhat to the reader.

It is desirable just here to devote a few pages to previous events immediately leading to what shall follow.

Everard Cushing Esq., Ralph's father, was, as may be supposed, a man of culture and property. Educated for the bar, at which he made a worthy *debut*; and for many years of active commercial habits, which he entered as more conducive to the health he lacked. His rapid successes, together with a growing distaste for the pursuits of commerce, had led to an early retirement. The age of fifty found him quite exempt from all bodily ailments and mental cares; established exactly to his mind at his fine country-seat among the highlands of the Hudson, near the pretty village of Apple Downs. In a manner the situation was quite aristocratic. His small family and his numerous household of servants were very properly under his absolute sway; and his estate was his kingdom. Horticulture, a fondness for all that is best in English literature; together with some business correspondence and the daily newspaper, had now filled up three years of a life in some sense entitled to rest, but in its strength and largeness were calculated for greater pursuits. He was beloved by his respected wife, and regarded with cold admiration by his well-provided children. He thought himself an affectionate husband and father; for, was not his wife his honored partner? And had not his son and his daughter the culture of Cushings, with the free range of the mansion?

Ralph was at this time twenty-two years old. Leaving college at twenty-one with no distinguished honors, but able to look back upon four years so well spent as to have endeared intellectual pursuits. His estimate of his own education was that it constituted a good beginning, — nothing more; a successful entrance upon larger regions that lay beyond. Hence one year of chafing against his father's will that he study law. His own wish was to study for a professorship abroad. A scene in the home library a few weeks before the occasion just related will give us the thread of events preceding, and bring us to our story again.

.   .   .   .

It was on a bright morning in August. Ralph, ever thoughtful for his mother, had passed a troubled night because of an unusual flush on her cheek the evening previous, and a too evident weariness in her patient eyes. He arose at the first hint of dawn, and found the heat of his anxiety really cooled by the exquisite freshness inhaled at that hour; and his unrested brain revived in beholding the transition from rosy tint to golden, that crept over the hills as the dawn advanced, as if a shower of rose-leaves, drawn into one seamless mantle, had spread over all and then passed sweetly, softly, without smell or hint of fire, into glorious, flaming light; consuming only darkness, and blessing all things waiting its benediction. Ralph sighed with pleasure, as under that benediction himself. And then his thoughts rose higher, while well-remembered words fell through his lips: 'Thou makest the outgoings of the morning and the evening to rejoice.' "Those words are good, but I only know them by heart," he said; "yet they seem to express more than ever."

And a half-mile walk, and then an encounter with William, who kept the lawn clipped and the orchards pruned, stirred up new and kindly thoughts until the weariness of the night was quite forgotten.

He re-entered the house on a summons to breakfast, his features having settled into an honest determination, as if some great thing to be achieved rested on himself. At breakfast Mr. Cushing was unusually genial. For this reason Mrs. Cushing was unusually happy, though so quietly that only Ralph's quick discernment noticed it. Ralph's sister Rebekah was strangely provoking, and Ralph was singularly silent. Indeed, the conduct of everybody was in some way exceptional; and Ralph, sure of his father's best mood, waited his opportunity. Half an hour after breakfast he entered the library where his father was sitting, and waited for him to look up.

"Sit down, Ralph," said Mr. Cushing. "You are on business, I see. Any European schemes agog?"

The young man bit his lip, but noticed the question in no other way; and said quietly,

"Father, I positively think that mother must go South for the winter, and go early. I do wish you would hear me through and look at it fairly."

Mr. Cushing made an impatient gesture. "Your mother is well enough, I think. She has several times lately told me that she feels very well. She looked unusually so this morning."

"Oh!" said Ralph, "mother is always very well when any one asks her how she does. Yes, she looked finely this morning; such invalids, who *never will* be invalids, always do, at times. But have you not noticed how much less her strength is within a few months? how quick her breathing becomes on any exertion? how unrefreshed she is in the morning? how indifferent her appetite? Happily, she has no cough; but I am sure this may lead to that, if neglected. What I think of most is, her great shrinking from cool weather, and her inability to meet it. The winters have been a severe trial to her constitution for five years past, and the next one will be worse borne than the last, depend upon it. She ought to be where she can have the open air, and the vision of something alive."

"Ralph, I knew you would make a good pleader. I still say what I have always said, that a lawyer you will make; and that you are fitted for nothing else, unless a preacher," he added, with a streak of bitter fun in his tone.

"No, father," said Ralph hotly, "not a lawyer, nor a preacher. I have no more religion than you have —— "

Mr. Cushing started, and so did Ralph; for, stung by his father's taunt, he had spoken precipitately, and without knowing how the words would sound.

"No," said his father, with the self-possessed dignity that always served him well. "No, Ralph, or *less*, perhaps; for I believe religion's first precept is of honor to one's father."

"Do you not see that you stung me, father?"

"And so you smote the wasp!"

"No,—sir! But overlook, forgive. Consider that in a cooler temper I would not have spoken so."

"Well, let it pass," said his father. " As for religion, more or less, it sets ill where found; so it is better missed."

"It sets well where it inheres," said Ralph, "but ill enough when assumed. Strange, since it signifies piety toward God, — strange that it should ever be assumed."

" Well, now, my noble son, sharp and solemn —the Bar or the Pulpit? But I did not mean to tease you again. You are sore to-day. Yes, it sets well where it interests, as with your mother, for instance," said Mr. Cushing, softening a little. "Ralph, it is well for you to care for your mother. She has been a faultless mother, as she has been an excellent wife. She has always graced my table, and provided well at my entertainments, and had an eye to my interests in every way. 'By their fruits ye shall know them' —an old maxim, proved true."

Ralph, whose color had been coming and going under this dubious eulogium of the mother he so dearly loved, nearly lost his self-possession here. "Was there ever an irony like this?" he thought; for one second, pale with the quick anger. But then, remembering that his father never opened the book from which he had unwittingly quoted, and knowing that he esteemed the one of whom he spoke, he replied collectedly, "I should say, father, that you have misapplied the maxim. But may I resume the subject with which I began?"

"Oh, Ralph, you bother me! Your mother is quite essential here; and, I am sure, is better off at home than she can be away. Besides, how *can* she go? Who for escort? and who for company? And what route fair enough for such a *very* great invalid?"

"Well, father, the first thing is your consent that she go. I dare say we may find a way and an escort."

"The doctor says her case is only one of nervous debility," said Mr. Cushing.

"What if it *is* only debility?" said Ralph, "she will be miserable all winter, and worse in the spring, with a constitution none the better for the trial. There is the point."

"Ralph, I must say I admire your concern for your mother, though I think you overdraw matters. And how can your mother be spared? Think of the Cushing mansion without Mrs. Cushing! But see me again about this after lunch, if you like. As you pass through the hall, strike two bells; I want to see William about those Bartletts; they are looking poorly. What have you ahead this morning?"

"Flowers for mother, and Rebekah for company."

"That will not fill up the morning. What next?"

Ralph seldom failed to talk his father into a talkative mood. "Rebekah's company has filled many a morning," said he, willing to prolong the scene, for he saw that he was working upon his father's better side. He could not agree with

him either in his selfishness or his prejudices;
but, trained by his mother's careful hand and
example, he felt that he could approach them
only in the way of entreaty and filial regard.

"A gallant speech!" said Mr. Cushing.
"Yes, Rebekah is a fine girl, — or *woman*.   How
old is the beauty?"

Now Rebekah Cushing was not beautiful, —
possessing only a lady-like figure and a fine
intellectual face of great plainness.   Ralph,
therefore, thought this too bad.   But he only
answered, "Twenty, yesterday."

"Really?" said his father; "I must see and
settle something on her soon.   After all, Ralph,
what next?"

"Blackstone, sir."

"What!"

"Blackstone, sir."

"Do I believe my ears?   I see you are in
earnest.   Indeed, you would not be a Cushing to
undertake anything lightly.   What has brought
you to this?"

"I suppose I may say mother's counsel, and — "

" That is," interrupted Mr. Cushing, half-sternly, " that is, your regard for your mother, and not your regard for your father!"

" I was about to add, sir, and my own conscience."

" Ah! then you confess you have been very wrong this year past."

Ralph did not confess that exactly. He felt that in a sense he had been in the right, and had been suffering wrong. And the dull, hopeless anguish of this new step, — as under the edge of his father's words he realized it a step actually taken, — he never undertook to weigh or estimate. He only knew that in his own experience it stood unprecedented and alone. Seeing that his father waited for an answer, he said, " Only in part, sir."

" Well, that is something. But your mother has always sided with you. What is the meaning of this new development? Mrs. Cushing is an honest woman, — a perfectly true woman."

"Mother has always been in sympathy with my preferences," said Ralph, "but never with any opposition to your will."

"I have no doubt you are right. Your mother has always trained her children as a Christian should; that is, as one should who professes what those people profess. Well, as I said, come again by-and-by. Don't forget to call William. I commend you to Rebekah and the florist; and, above all, to Blackstone."

Mr. Cushing was possessed of one of those strong, eccentric natures that are somewhat characterized by marked contrasts. Too really noble to be chargeable with any meanness, he was not so absolutely strong as to be free from weakness; nor were mind and heart so well disciplined as to be truly Catholic. In fact, his weak points numbered several, and his prejudices not less than two or three. He was not open to every kind of flattery, but he was some times flattered by the most guileless conduct on the part of others. His authority, the law of his own will, he above all things worshipped; and any new discovery of its weight and importance filled him with inexpressible satisfaction. The only good that this ever worked to any one, was in the quiet glow for the time emanating from it toward all his lowly subjects. It was thus he found himself in the midst of a kindly reverie as to whether Mrs. Cushing could possibly be spared, when William entered. And William thought his master had never been so gracious before, nor so easy in his requisitions, nor half so commendatory of the care exhibited in the pear orchard, notwithstanding the poor-looking Bartletts.

CHAPTER III.

REBEKAH.

WHEN Ralph left the library he sought Rebekah, who was waiting for him impatiently, but well occupied as usual. She was rambling through *Cosmos* to find something satisfactory about meteors; and, quite in despair both of the meteors and of Ralph, she exclaimed on his entering the pretty study and sewing-room, " Ralph, dear, where have you been? You come like a comet, at long intervals; but all unexpectedly, like one of those provoking aerolites. That is, nobody can compute your movements, and nobody knows very

(32)

much about you, — at least nobody but mamma and I. Dear me! I don't believe anybody does know what meteors are, nor what this August shower of fire means. But you are a fixed star of the first magnitude. What *are* meteors, Ralph? and what is the meaning of all this fuss in the sky lately?"

Ralph laughed heartily at this outburst, and especially at the idea of being at once comet, meteor, and fixed star.

"There! I knew you would laugh at me," continued Rebekah, "you always do."

"I always *don't*, dear sister, — you sweet, provoking sister! Take that back, please do!"

"You never laugh at me maliciously, brother, — only sublimely and sweetly, as a star may at anything terrestrial. But I am quite willing to let you laugh at me this time, if only to give your face a pleasant expression. You looked so unsubmissively doleful when you came in. I am sure you have not gained your cause."

"What cause?" asked their mother, looking

up from some embroidery that was making haste to be ready for the *trousseau* of friend Hopefield's daughter, Faith, who was to be married to Ethelred Summers, Mr. Cushing's head florist. All the household knew that Mrs. Cushing scorned to be idle, and that she lost nothing of position or dignity in contributing by some exertion to the happiness of every member.

"Oh, that is a great secret, mamma," said Rebekah and Ralph, in their haste speaking together.

"But," continued Rebekah, "it is no secret that we are going down to the green-house to get every kind of flower that doesn't make your head ache. We may bring orange-flowers, I know."

"A few, very few, dear, for me, — and at a tolerable distance."

"Then you don't want them in your hair?"

"No," said her mother, laughing, "I want them before my eyes. The beauty must be seen to make the fragrance perfect."

" Oh, sweet philosopher-poet, mamma! Who can ever love you enough? Now Ralph, let us go, and you shall tell me about meteors."

But the conversation fell on other subjects, just then all-absorbing to Ralph. As they went out, he took up Rebekah's last words to their mother. " Mamma is more than philosopher, or poet, or both," he said. " When she was reading with us this morning, and came upon the verse, ' Who shall tell thee words whereby thou and all thy house shall be saved,' her voice was like a prayer, but a prayer triumphant. But have you ever heard anything read as she read the psalm afterward? ' Oh, Lord God of my salvation, I have cried day and night before Thee.' It seemed as if she were close in the audience of a friend; only of one very, very far above — one that may be worshipped. I half think she forgot that we were there. And I quite know that we have a wonderful mother."

Rebekah was silent, — half-rebuked for her own harmless bantering; in full sympathy with

Ralph, and too nearly tearful to respond. Ralph continued : —

"I have sometimes fancied that we are all safe, all insured for the hereafter, because of mother's faith and faithful living. But of course this would be a perversion of those words, thou and all thy house.' It must be a personal matter with every one. Mother *has* something that *I have not*, and which is not in her gift. You have the same; I don't doubt you have. But then it is a younger, weaker thing with you. You are less settled and less happy. I am *un*settled and *un*happy."

"Oh, Ralph, brother!" exclaimed Rebekah gently, "You overcome one's judgment, one's self-possession, with your tremendous emotions. I did not know you were this way, though I have noticed you as very attentive when mamma reads. I am glad you have expressed this. There will certainly be a good end. And if I don't know very well how to help you, there is something very satisfactory, very sweet, in feeling

perfectly sure that God understands your difficulties better than I can. There must be an infinite depth of compassion in His infinite heart."

" I have no doubt there is," answered Ralph.
" But how do you know there will certainly be
a good end ? Many pass through these storms
only to strike on a shoal."

" Rebekah was thoughtful for a moment, and
then said, " The certainty is not *in you*, of
course."

They had been prolonging their walk through
the grounds, and Ralph here remembered that
they were getting no nearer the green-houses.
Accordingly they turned down a short walk
leading to the lawn, on the other side of which
lay a slope toward the south, where the green-
houses were.

" Orange-flowers are very well," said Ralph,
" and indeed I did not mean to speak so coldly.
They are superb, delicious, exquisite, and all
that sort of thing. But I like them most of all
untouched, in their old habit on the trees. That

way we get the white flashing among the dark green, and the fragrance diffused into finer tone and less palling richness. It is as if they filled all the space between sky and earth, with just as much as one can well sustain of the perfection of perfumes."

"You are like mamma," said Rebekah; "you must *see* them, and not too near. But one can have them in your chosen way only at the South. I wonder if mamma will go this year?"

"Mamma," said Ralph, "likes nothing so completely as a perfect rose, half-blown, and on a single spray. It may be pink, or any shade of red, or it may be white; but not ash or straw color."

"White japonicas for me!" said Rebekah.

"Sister!" exclaimed Ralph, "you are twenty years old, and I never knew that before! For once I sorrowfully disagree with you."

"*Why*, Ralph?"

"Oh, they *weary* me! They are like some impassive human flowers that one sees here and there, — painfully exquisite, horribly inexpressive ; voiceless, passionless, soulless. Interrogate them ; they yield nothing. A pillar of salt were better."

"Ralph! How singular! Japonicas are universally esteemed to stand well among things of beauty. It seems to me they fill their own place there richly, not inexpressively. And so, for once, *I* am quite glad to disagree with *you*. My own declaration would still be that japonicas are delightful. So clear and strong on their stem, — no suggestion either of weakness or of self-consciousness or assumption. But the idea of bringing metaphysical analysis to bear on flowers! Ralph, you are spoiling me! But no!" she said quickly, catching a kiss, "no! I did not mean that. You *help* me. Nevertheless, I like japonicas, the white especially. Brilliancy and fragrance are only qualities, and give their own expression in their own place."

"I believe," said Ralph, "that the rose and the lily are the only flowers mentioned in the Bible."

"I never thought of that," said Rebekah. " I suppose they characterized the fields and hill-sides of that country where the Bible was writ-ten. 'Shall He not much more clothe you, O ye of little faith?' How sweet, oh, how sweet that is! Better than our analysis. We get some *truths* mingled in with our philosophies. But that loving One of Bethlehem, and Galilee, and Bethany; of Gethsemane and Olivet,—gave us *the truth;* and *is* the Truth."

And Ralph said " Yes," as one dreaming, not knowing what he said. It was a " yes" in which there was neither confession nor assent.

They found Ethelred busy as ever among the forest of flowers and exotic green in the apart-ment devoted to tropical plants. Hotter than ever, Rebekah thought it, almost drenching as it was with the sweet earthy vapor that held in itself a mingling of all choice odors. But every-thing looked so well arranged and so perfectly thriving, so luxuriantly happy, that she could not help complimenting Ethelred on his skill and diligence. "It is wonderful how much there is to do, and how well you do it, Ethel. You are always busy, and always in good order. Oh, Ethel! my mother says that you shall have plenty of flowers for the wedding. And you must get some pots ready, besides, with what Faith will best like to have in the cottage win-dow."

"Thank you, *mum*," said the young Scotch-man, his fine, honest face lighting up with a satisfied and grateful pleasure. "Mistress Cushing never forgets any one. Is my lady well this morning?"

"Oh, we hope she is pretty well, Ethel. This is too warm for me, and I don't find what I want most. So, Ralph, I am going to the warm regions of the temperate zone. You can find me, I dare say, when you have enough of this."

Ralph said, "Yes, presently," and fell upon Ethelred with such a volley of questions about all manner of plants and shrubs, and trees, too, for that matter, that the good fellow resigned all other employment to give the desired information. With all Ralph's delight in flowers, botany had never been a favorite study with him, and plain Ethelred had always seemed to him marvellous with his long, unpronounceable names for everything. Satisfied at length, for the time, but still in an inquisitive vein, he suddenly asked, " Ethel, how came a sturdy Scot like you by a name all Saxon ? "

The florist, who was ill at ease outside the element of his special .calling, looked puzzled; and Ralph relieved him by saying pleasantly, " The kings Ethelred were good fellows, I dare say, and there is reason enough that you be their namesake. Quite likely Faith can tell you about them. If she is as good at housekeeping as you are at flower-tending, the cottage will be a royal cottage, — I venture as good as the first Ethelred's palace."

All this time Ethel was cutting flowers here

and there, as Ralph pointed out. His respectful, intelligent look met Ralph's clear eyes, as he said: " Mr. Ralph, the sunlight, and heat, and moisture, reaching the lily-principle or rose-principle, or whatever may be in seed, or cutting, or bulb, bring into action what God has stored up there ; and, as the parson at the kirk would say, ' develop the divine ideas of life and beauty.' Of course, sir, we find our honest labors prospered ; that is part of the ordering. But every day I find the happy thought that it's not me that makes all these things to flourish. It's only Him. And His name's wonderful."

Ralph remembered the other words, — "Counsellor, the Mighty God, the Everlasting Father, the Prince of Peace." And, as he answered kindly, " You are quite right, Ethel," he found himself wondering if those names standing in prophecy really pointed to Jesus; and how any one could be sure of it. And then he thought with himself further: " The person who appeared to Manoah in the field had the same name. Could it be that this one and the one who afterward, as St. John says, 'was made flesh and dwelt among us,' was the same person? And then, *who is* the person? Paul's tone is that of conviction, actual knowledge, when he declares that the Rock of Israel, in their wilderness days, was Christ."

Such thoughts were not unusual with Ralph, and they were nowise hindered, but rather strengthened by the enjoyment of the hour. He was nearly ready to express them to Ethel, and to ask his views, when Rebekah appeared with a playful rebuke for leaving her alone so long. And, bidding Ethel be sure to let them know as soon as the day was fixed, she carried Ralph off without ceremony, " because mamma was certainly weary with embroidery, and with waiting for them."

" Ralph dear," she said, as they entered the house, " I am not sure that I am less settled or less happy than mamma. Religious life is certainly, as you suppose, a younger and a weaker thing with me, and far more lacking. This must be because there has been less personal acquaintance with the Saviour, both in converse and in suffering. But I am quite settled as to who Jesus is, and what He has done for me. The home-nest is *there*, you know; the happiness is *there*."

CHAPTER IV.

FEARS FOR THE MOTHER.

RALPH went off by himself to read Blackstone, and Rebekah to "embroider mamma," as she called the adorning of her mother's person and apartment with flowers. The morning passed off busily with all, and the lunch pleasantly. Mr. Cushing was remarkably silent, for his habit at table was conversational, or, if we must be accurate, *dictatorial*. He was fond of hearing himself talk; and, it must be allowed that he was generally entertaining to others. On this occasion he was, as sometimes happened, so indisposed to speak that others could be heard without interruption. To-day he was grave and genial by turns, unusually responsive to Mrs. Cushing's remarks, and, in fact, seemed to take pleasure in listening to others rather than himself.

As was customary for the first hour after lunch, all withdrew to the library. Mr. Cushing placed himself for his usual nap on the old, high-backed lounge, lulled by Rebekah's voice reading to him selections from the Iliad. Ralph said the mother must have a nap by all means. But the mother, as usual, " did not need it at all." She would take her sewing, and talk with Ralph, and they could listen to Rebekah at the same time.

" Now mamma," said Ralph, " if you can sew, and converse, and listen to reading all at one time, there must be something the matter with you; your faculties are abnormally elevated. The homœopathic dictation would be mesmerism, if maxims be followed. Now that you are well placed in the big chair, I shall stroke your hair awhile, and you shall talk to me, but neither sew nor listen to reading. Those Greek fables are so tiresome!"

"Ralph, my scholarly Ralph! where is your classic taste?"

"Oh, it is the ideal that is classic, not the real. It is the imaginative language — the Homeric diction, at once stalwart and graceful — the sustained energy of the whole as a poem, that gives beauty to the narrative. Strip the story bare of all that is Homeric, and you have left a very ugly series of bloody wars and coarse adventures hardly good to read of. The only benefit the world has received from the Iliad is its contribution to language. The same seems to me true of all the heathen classics, — at least measurably so. They have enriched vastly the linguistic fertility and taste of modern times, — real thought and historic lore in a less degree."

"Well, Ralph, quite likely you are right," said his mother; "I never did see that the moral tone is elevated or the heart enriched by anything in heathen literature. Yet the mere knowledge of language, and the mental discipline acquired in putting good Greek or Latin into good English, must have done the race, intellectually, a vast service."

"Yes," said Ralph, "I suppose anything that tends to develop the individual and enlarge his usefulness, must be to the glory of God. But, if our developed faculties worship themselves, or are spoiled by their own philosophy — " He paused and left the sentence unfinished, not wishing to start a conversation that might disturb his mother. Presently he added : " And then, so far as we can see, if there had been no Alexandria, no Italy, no Art, and a loss to science beside."

"You have all those historic links in man's progress far more accurately in your mind than I have," said his mother, "and no doubt you could make a strong case. My own first thought would be that that which more than anything else has originated action as well as thought,

4

tending to man's present elevation, is the human life of Christ, and His living Gospel. But God has built the whole present, or the whole past. Every bit of the under-structure has its value."

Ralph was silent so long that his mother at length asked him how he had gotten on with his law-reading.

"Shall I say just what I want to say?" asked Ralph.

" Why, yes, I suppose so," said his mother, opening her eyes that were really growing sleepy under Ralph's persistent stroking.

" Well, then, I *hate* it!" said he reluctantly.

" What! The Trojans are coming, Cassandra!" exclaimed Mr. Cushing starting up, and then, more ashamed than sleepy, lapsing into his nap again.

Ralph's manœuvre was so successful that his mother was soon asleep also, and Rebekah, who had ceased reading, beckoned him to come over to her corner. She had yet had nothing from him as to the conversation with his father in the

morning, and was impatient to hear about it
They withdrew to the verandah to avoid all the
risk of being overheard. For although there
was nothing in principle to conceal, and they
were never disposed to secrecy towards their
parents, yet the time seemed not yet ripe for
broaching the subject with the family assembled.
Ralph rehearsed as much as was expedient of
the morning's conversation, and each thought
that their father had been remarkably forbear-
ing. They felt sure, also, that if he could only
be convinced of the advisability of the proposed
step, he would coincide in everything.

" But I do think, Ralph," said his sister, " that
your plan of sending me with mamma is not the
best one, nor even a good one. Papa must have
somebody to fill mamma's place, as far as that is
possible, — to look over his linen, to preside at
table, to look after Jane and Joan in a hundred
matters, and all that. After a few weeks there
will be very little company at Apple Downs
until June; but think of any friend coming to

pass day or evening, and no lady in the house! We must not forget father while we consider mother."

Ralph saw the truth and right of all this, but felt that the mother needed Rebekah more, saying, " And papa could be a good deal in the city; and when at home would do very well with me."

" Oh, Ralph, dear, do you not see it wouldn't do? You are the one to go with mamma, and I, if either, can keep papa's house. The house must be kept, you know. Whatever plans papa may make, he never will plan to be of the party himself. He dislikes the South, and detests travelling."

Rebekah always gave good reasons, and gave them honestly. Sometimes (and wisely enough) she did not give them all, unless they were asked. In this instance, she felt very strongly that Ralph would have more than his usual need of their mother's presence, and influence, at this juncture of his life; and also, that the responsibility of caring for her would be good for him. Ralph, however, asked for no further reasons. He only said, "We are talking as if mamma's going were decided upon. Do you really think father will come to it?"

"Oh, I think so," said Rebekah. "Papa likes to do the proper thing. But don't say or do anything imprudent, Ralph."

"Rebekah!" said their father, appearing on the verandah at that moment, and catching the last words, "if the round world were as prudent as you are, every year would be a cycle. If the human kind never did anything at a venture, there would be few great things done. What are you berating Ralph for?"

Ralph drew back somewhat at this sudden outburst, but Rebekah answered quietly, and with a sweet frankness that characterized her so well, "Ah, papa! if you couldn't 'berate' your perverse daughter for her prudence, now and then, you would miss of a very healthful excitement. It is good for you to scold me, papa,

—you always kiss me afterward. Since Ralph has been telling me of his conversation with you this morning, I suppose I may explain that I was begging him to say nothing imprudently; that is, nothing that could in any way disturb you. I think he feels with me that he has said all he can fitly say, and that nothing more can be said except by you."

"Only," said Ralph, "by your permission, father, I was to introduce the subject again this afternoon."

"You or I were to introduce it," said Mr. Cushing. "I said, 'see me again on the subject.' Well, let us all see each other about it. Come in, you two young ones!"

Ralph's heart leaped with such a bound that he happily did not hear the last two words, for they would have nettled him sorely. "What can have inclined father so soon toward this?" he thought. "Is it possible that miserable *Law* can have worked such a benefit?"

Their mother had resumed her sewing, and,

all unconscious of being waited on by a deputation, greeted them with her usual quiet pleasantry. " Well, children, is father bringing you in, or are you bringing him in ? "

The conversation that followed was long and animated. The mother was at first unable to comprehend that the whole family were enlisted in a plan for wintering her at the South, before she was even aware of a thought in that direction. Mr. Cushing's dictation was less violent and more kindly than usual, but still in sufficient keeping with his general habit to make the others feel sure they were not dreaming. Her own acquiescence was the only point now to be gained, and it is not strange that she was less submissive than her wont; for how could she be so victimized by kindness as to be disturbed out of her loved and quiet home ?

" But you are not the victim of anybody's kindness, mamma," said Ralph. " Only be the loyal subject of expediency. Do the pruaent thing, so that you may have t^h ebetter health, —

possibly confirmed health,— for the next winter at home."

Ralph got himself laughed at by all for this prudent speech. Mrs. Cushing, who had never been away from home and family except for her annual visit of a few weeks to her own mother in New England, felt very strongly that she could not go away. Since her mother's death, and their own removal from somewhat fashion- able life in New York to their country home, she had indulged to the full her strong attach- ment to the simple routine of domestic life and neighborly visitation, giving only a few enter- tainments to Mr. Cushing's city friends, and other visitors during the summer; and one or two of a plainer sort in the winter to their imme- diate neighbors. She had fondly thought that here she should abide undisturbed. The twen- ty-five years of her married life had been fully assured of her husband's honest-hearted esteem, and of the value in which he held her presence; notwithstanding the habitual lack of that considerateness which she had always sought and always missed. She was thus quite sure that it was at a kind of self-sacrifice that he was now propounding a scheme for her relief from the fatigue of home cares and the trial of a northern winter. And indeed it was so. He was quite sure the house would go to ruin without her. But his finer traits had been somewhat aroused, and he based his proposition on the ground that, although he had not noticed the recent decline in her strength, yet he did remember that she was ill two or three times the last winter and the winter preceding, and how Doctor Saywell had suggested that her constitution was ill-adapted to the winter climate of the North and East. "Go South, and go Westward," he said. And though Mrs. Cushing had been apparently so well all the last five months, yet certainly she was not in as good flesh as in the beginning of the autumn a year ago. It would be better to take matters in season. The coming winter might make greater inroads on her health than the last.

Mrs. Cushing begged that the subject might be laid aside, and canvassed again after a little reflection.

At breakfast next morning, the discussion was resumed. Southward and westward, Ralph said, would suit exactly, for there were cousins in Ohio, cousins in Tennessee, and cousins in Louisiana. They could easily cross Kentucky and Mississippi without cousining. There was no way of making a long journey pleasantly, except by stages; and his mamma's cousin Cecilia had repeatedly urged her to give them a good long visit.

"Ralph," said his father, "you are a true Cushing, and your idea only needs elaboration to make it practical. You dislike to travel by railway, Helen," he said, addressing his wife; "and my thought is, that keeping Ralph for company as was planned yesterday, you make the most of your opportunities, and travel in the very easiest and most beneficial way, that is, in our own carriage. Zedekiah and the horses are very little needed at home in the winter; and for the autumn, William can turn groom, and the gray colt will have the chance to prove his qualities. This will give you the additional advantage of your private carriage for your own, and your friends' convenience during your visits. But such a plan would necessitate starting soon, and proceeding slowly."

Rebekah clapped her hands at this delightful arrangement. Mr. Cushing was constitutionally disposed to do a thing handsomely if he did it at all; and in a way somewhat original and striking. In this instance, it was in a way very agreeable to all concerned. Mrs. Cushing acknowledged that she should enjoy travelling in that way, and that it would be pleasant to visit Cecilia Stanley. She suggested, however, that Doctor Saywell be spoken to. It seemed a very serious undertaking to leave home for so long a time, and so soon, but if he considered it of any importance, she would make up her mind to it, and to all the enjoyment of it.

Ralph declared that if his father pleased, nobody but he should ask the doctor to call. " Then we will write to all the cousins, and be ready to start as soon as we get replies," he said.

" Be sure you take plenty of law-books," said his father quizzically.

" My poor sister! will not you have a hard time, though ? " said Ralph, as they passed through the hall together

" Oh no, Ralph, never fear," she answered. " It will be so strengthening and joy-giving to think of sweet little mother having a good time *all the time*, and of your being less provoked and more happy, as you always are with her. I expect papa to be quite in love with my presidency."

" Did you mean ' more happy' or more submissive ? " he asked half bitterly.

" Submission brings happiness, when it is a right submission," she answered, as they entered their mother's room for the reading.

CHAPTER V.

PREPARATIONS FOR THE JOURNEY.

OCTER SAYWELL called duly, and reiterated his former suggestion with additional emphasis. Mrs. Cushing had certainly lost ground since he last saw her, and would almost certainly not endure the coming winter as well as the last. He said exactly enough in that direction; and then all manner of frank, honest, kindly things in praise of the journey and of the method chosen; and in the way of encouragement that the winter would thus be passed without drawbacks, and that another year might find her quite able —— or, at least, much *better* able — to remain at home. And as he took leave, with his cheery laugh, cautioning against too long daily stages, and against driving after sun-down except on warm evenings and guarded by quinine, Mrs. Cushing felt quite fortified for the undertaking.

The letters were written, and the various preparations entered upon step by step. Jane the cook, and her sister Joan the housemaid, and William's wife Margaret the laundress, were loud in their lamentations that Mistress Cushing should leave them for so long. "And what would master do? and that sweet young thing, Miss Rebekah?" — Margaret could not bear to think that her bairns might be sick, and Mrs. Cushing away — "she was always so good in sickness, and so kind-like at all times." Indeed, Zedekiah the coachman, or 'Zed' as he was pleased to be called, was the only member of the domestic retinue who seemed perfectly delighted at the arrangement. It would be a wonderful thing to see so much of the country; and he regarded it in the light of a promotion that he should be entrusted with the driving of freight so precious and honorable, and through so many dangers as they must encounter in all those hundreds of miles. He would be sure to have Penn and Philip in extraordinarily fine order for the start — "and wouldn't they look well, entering strange towns with their fine trappings?"

And truly, the horses were handsome, well-kept animals; sufficiently " splendid " to attract admiration anywhere. Their names were a conceit of Ralph's; well matched as to size and color, and outline, they yet presented marked contrasts in disposition; Philip of Macedon, having when left to himself, a martial tread and an untamed eye, was given to snorting, pawing and usurpation. William Penn, on the other hand, was as gentle as he was handsome, and fleet and strong.

It was the twelfth of August; and, as the chosen method of travel would be impracticable after the days became decidedly cool, it was arranged to start so unprecedentedly early as the third of September, in order to accomplish their Ohio visit, and get well on their way southward by the first of October.

The three weeks slipped quickly away, — all too quickly poor Rebekah thought; and so thought every one except Ralph and the visionary Zed. One after another the looked-for letters came in, complimenting Mr. Cushing on his liberal invention, and full of cordiality toward the proposed visits. "Cousin Cecilia" was particularly overflowing. "Safety, speed, and comfort," she wrote, "are three words that make a phrase in all railway advertisements now-a-days. And where speed is essential, as it generally is in this hey-day world, the second word is the great thing of beauty in men's eyes. But I say put *benefit* for 'speed,' and couple 'safety' and 'comfort' with that veracious adjective *absolute*, and you have the perfection of travelling. Where is this to be found dear Helen but in one's own family carriage? — supposing the horses to be gentle, the driver reliable, the harness perfect, the wheels quite secure, and everything exactly as it should be; neither flaw, nor jar, nor apprehension of hindrance. In the present instance all this is quite supposable: for Mr. Cushing, I know, is a man of all others to have everything absolute in its way."

Cousin Cecilia had a sparkle of fun in her constitution, but she had also her absolute qualities, and one of these was *sincerity.* All who knew her at all, knew this. And, as suspicion was not one of Mr. Cushing's weaknesses, the unfair thought happily did not occur to him, that this good creature might possibly be quizzing him, just a very little and quite charitably.

A great deal was done in those three weeks of preparation, and an unwonted degree of diligent care was awakened on the part of all the servants, to have everything exactly right for mistress during her too brief delay before the long farewell, so that what had always been done cheerfully and well was now done superlatively. The cooking had never been so faultlessly exact, nor so skilfully varied and elaborate; the carpets had never been so accurately swept, nor every speck of dust spied out so ruthlessly by Joan, without a hint from anyone; the linen had never been quite so snowy or so glossy before, nor so carefully laid away. And with all the natural excitement and disturbance occasioned by the great event, the house had never been more quiet, nor had Mr. Cushing ever been so nearly affectionate towards his wife since the first six months of their wedded life, as during the last two of these three eventful weeks. On two occasions he actually accompanied the family from breakfast to the little drawing-room, and begged the mother to go on with the customary reading as if he were not there, — a direction in the form of a request, with which she was hardly able to comply for too much joy.

One day near sunset, in the last week of that glad, yet half-sad time of preparation, Ralph who had been vexing his soul with the irksome law-study and was not yet quite in a perfect mood, sat leaning out of his western window, indulging in certain reflections, longings and aspirations of which no one but himself has ever known the exact purport. The last hour had been a pleasant one, though not quite filling to his satisfaction, the vacant place that somehow he could never get filled. He had just returned from driving his mother and sister in the light phaeton over to friend Hopefield's, to say a kindly farewell to them all, and especially to Faith, whose wedding couldn't possibly be made to come off before October, and she must be excused if the tears did start with the vain regret that Mrs. Cushing could not ornament it with her presence, and warm it with her fresh, kind salutations.

Ralph always enjoyed these drives, and this evening he had particularly enjoyed the society of his two companions, which, — like the familiar landscape, never shifting, yet always in some way changing and newly suggestive, — had en·

livened him greatly for the time. But, for all
this, he had returned only to take up again the
burden of his vexed and tired mood; not de-
jected, but weary and reflective, he allowed a
shade of the vexation in the tone with which he
answered a rap at his door, but uttered an excla-
mation of glad welcome as Rebekah entered.

"Not tired of me yet, patient brother?" she
asked gayly, as she stepped forward to his win-
dow-seat.

"Oh, sister, no; I am sure you don't think
I am or can be tired of you. But I am not
'patient,' not a bit so. Sit down, you rest me
already."

She sat down, waiting for him to say more;
only stroking his hand fondly, and once saying
how much their mamma had enjoyed the drive
and the call, these Hopefields were so simple
and intelligent.

"Rebekah," said Ralph after a long gaze of
enjoyment at the glowing sunset, in which he
knew she was participating, "did you know that

you omitted Calvary? I mean the other day when we talked, walking through the grounds, and you spoke of Christ as the One of Gethsemane and Olivet."

" I hoped you would have noticed it, and am glad you have," said Rebekah. " Indeed, I have felt so sure that you would resume our talk of that happy morning before you and mamma leave, that I have been quite safe in waiting for you. Yes, I purposely omitted Calvary then, because I was thinking especially of our Saviour's human living and teaching ; or rather, the Divine teaching of His human lips and life ; of how he was made flesh, and *dwelt among us.* The fulness of grace and truth were manifested before the precious blood was shed. There was suffering in the *life*, there was sorrow in the *living* heart ; but it was all the necessary condition of a living fellowship with the Father in this world- that hated the Father, and of the devotion to the work He had, in the form of a servant, undertaken for His afflicted and poor people.   There was sacrifice in this Divine opportunity, well fulfilled; of Divine greatness in humilation; of becoming the patient ingatherer of His own flock, and opening their minds to the truth, their hearts to Himself.   In all this there was sacrifice.   But in the blood-shedding was *redemption*, and more than redemption, — *atonement!* for the heart apprehending the death of Christ as He himself does, is *at one* with Him forevermore."

Again Ralph made no immediate reply; and when he did speak he only said somewhat abruptly, " Oh, I have heard *endless* sermons on these subjects; some of them very sweetly and manfully spoken, by men who were intellectually strong, and no doubt speaking their convictions and living by them.   All I can say is that, in my own *belief*, I am no where in particular; except that I am sure there is something in Christ that *I want*."

Rebekah did not know what to say.   She knew that God had taught her own heart, but she was not sure of her ability to teach another. She spoke soon, saying gently, "It is not only *something in* Him that you want, or need. You need *Him;* and your want, or longing, will be filled when you possess Him. He did not give something that He *had* or *was* for us. He gave *Himself* for us."

" Well " said Ralph, " I dare say you say well, but I do not understand it. I remember your expression of the other day — '*personal acquaintance with the Saviour.*' I can realize that there may be a divine, unseen, everywhere present Person — such an one as mother seems acquainted with, and seems to be always within reach of. But then, if the 'possessing' of which you speak lies in a *getting*, how am I to get or lay claim to the Person as possessed acquaintance, friend, saviour ? The getting, certainly does not come by *reformation ;* I have seen reformed men, and moral men, who needed no reforming ; *spotless* men, in their own eyes, and before any human tribunal. I have admired and disliked them about equally.   I never could feel that they had Christ."

" Oh, Ralph dear," said Rebekah, " it is not getting, it is receiving."

There was no impatience in the tone in which Ralph replied ; " I don't understand the one any better then the other, sister.   But everything you say carries the conviction that you are not mistaken."   Then, after a moment of silence he added, " You did not answer my question the other day."

" What question ? "

" You were certain there would be a good end to this unsettledness, — these difficulties and questionings — and I asked you how you knew."

Rebekah laughed her sweet, natural laugh. There was nothing in it that could irritate or wound.   " I tried to answer you," she said. " What was it ?   Oh, yes !   I said that the certainty was not in you.   Of course it could not be.   There is nothing certain in any of us."

" You can't persuade me," said Ralph, " that

that answered the question, nor that you think it did. Your mind works too accurately to dupe itself that way."

Rebekah laughed again. She could not help it. But seeing that Ralph could not exactly join her, she let herself again into the stronger mood. "You are concerned about the issue," she said, "because you are looking at everything from your own unsettled stand-point, and the largest, most reliable party believed in is your uncertain self."

Ralph started. Did Rebekah say that? And was that really true? But he only said, "Well, the question is not answered yet."

Rebekah continued: "If I thought you under some vague excitement, or actuated by some definite calculation of self-interest, I should not be at all happy as to the probable result, because I should not be at all sure that God were leading you to Himself, — only that you were yourself endeavoring to impel yourself into some sort of a religious life. But it is quite plain that God is doing with you what He always does with a soul that He is determined to subdue and lift up.   He is making you *hungry for Him.* The hand of Christ has touched your heart, and discovered to you its weakness, its emptiness.   But you are thereby *wedded to* that hand.   Its touch drew you, and awoke you into eagerness, — thoughtful, abiding, real, — to know and live with the heart that animates and moves that bruising, healing touch.   You are thirsty for the living God.   And," she said, putting up her face to his, all radiant with sisterly pride, affection, and yearning, " it almost seems that you are beginning to drink."

He bent over and let her kiss him, but did not answer her by word or sign, save that one. They sat until the twilight deepened.   Then Ralph said they must look for their mother. " You must have all of mamma that you can while she is at home," he said.   And as they rose to go, he told Rebekah that her last word had brought to his mind the words of Jesus:

If any man thirst, let him come unto me and drink. "Are you perfectly sure that the living God is *there?*" he asked.

"Perfectly sure!" she answered, "and you will not rest until you are sure also."

CHAPTER VI.

FRIENDLY GATHERINGS.

ONE of the last things to be accomplished before the final departure, was an evening entertainment to the remnant of "city company" that remained so late at Apple Downs, and to the few resident grandees who were able to feel at home on the Brussels and velvet of the mansion. To Mrs. Cushing and Rebekah this was partly an imperative ceremony to be begun, conducted, and finished according to Mr. Cushing's most exact ideas; partly a pleasant and congenial mode of expressing their cordial interest in their acquaintances, and their unwillingness to omit this opportunity of giving them a pleasant evening and a bright farewell. As for Ralph, he liked these occurrences well enough while they lasted, and was very glad when they were well over. He was quite able to be the life of any company, but was more content to be looking out the two or three choice spirits of the company, with whom he could interchange thought as well as animation. Of animation, however, Ralph had a large fund, and his absence from any circle where he was known, was always a presence missed, — as was the case on this eventful evening, for the short and simple reason that Ralph had a headache. Miss Celestina Rubens, who sought to rival her illustrious namesake with paint and brush, was especially disappointed that Ralph was not to be seen, because she wished his " valued opinion " as to sundry points in her art where opinions might differ. She had decided to remain in the country a month later than usual, in order to sketch in water colors "the best scenes of the season," which she could then copy in oil at her longest leisure.　Miss Celestina had brought a miniature landscape, done in oil colors, all the way from the Rubens farm, to present to Mrs. Cushing, if Rebekah thought it would "do;" a most happy phrase, allowing the martyr critic to say, "Oh, by all means — perfectly well," without the least hesitation; and then, of her own voluntary pleasure, to invent certain kind and truthful expressions, in order that the aspiring *article* might escape the slightest wound of misgiving that her sorry daub was not in every possible way acceptable.　Miss Rubens, who was as generally disinterested as she was simple, was thus quite bereft of all concern on the subject. Her face lighted up much as the face of one born blind may become expanded and quickened under a discourse about the sun, and she was able to pass the evening quite comfortably, notwithstanding Ralph's absence, — declaring that, when the evening star had set, there was no use expecting it to rise till the world had turned over again.

Mrs. Cushing moved among her guests with the ease, and fine carriage, and quick perception of which her husband was so proud, and with the benevolent eye and unaffected gesture so inseparable from her nature. Both host and hostess were admirable in their sphere, noticing the in-coming of each new guest, greeting each with genuine grace and cordiality, never wanting in suitable words of welcome, and making some pleasant introductions for all. With all this, each was moving here and there to see that all were well entertained; occasionally forming new groups, or starting new themes.

While Rebekah was still entertaining Miss Celestina, and a few other young ladies and gentlemen, Mr. Livermore Maxwell was discoursing to Mr. Cushing's great amusement, of the improved state and style of restaurants in New York since he was a boy,— forty years then gone.   And the same gentleman proceeded to edify Mr. Wunderman with an amazing amount of eloquence on the inadequacy of railroad projections to meet the wants of the country; the like inadequacy of investments for the work in hand, and the deficiency of stone bridges, and of engineering generally.

Doctor Saywell was there, of course; and was overheard to say that the Cushings entertained better than anybody in the country.   The sorest trial of the evening to Mrs. Cushing (except the wine, which Mr. Cushing had imperatively voted in) was a long disquisition from Matthew Drawdeep, Esq., on the significance of the times, and the important moral lessons to be deduced from recent political and social events.   Mr. Drawdeep was Superintendent of the Sunday School in Mr. Hidden's church; and he expressed his conviction that the children should be instructed more by the moral import of passing facts, and the analogies of nature, than from "the letter of the Gospel,"—a phrase that was quite new to Mrs. Cushing. She extricated herself at last, pitying the Sunday School children very much, and pitying herself a little, that she had been obliged to be polite to Mr. Drawdeep, for at least ten minutes, when her presence was essential elsewhere.

When the company dispersed, Miss Celestina with commendable adroitness, found just the right opportunity to present her "oil sketch" to Mrs. Cushing who, in her sincere regard for the good young lady, had no difficulty whatever in accepting it, in a manner that gave the giver greater pleasure than her own best execution could possibly have done in itself. The ever true and ever perfect *word of the Lord Jesus,* that it is more blessed to give than to receive, was doubly exemplified in this instance. There was superlative blessing on each side ; because, as each received, each gave, cordially, sincerely, if not equally.

.   .   .   .

But it was not enough for Mrs. Cushing that

6

her friends and her rich neighbors had received some expression of her husband's society views and her own good-will. She could not be satisfied without the added pleasure of an entertainment that should bring in many of her esteemed and valued neighbors, who would not have felt at home in the gathering first assembled. To this Mr. Cushing made no objection. He liked to have his house thrown open; and if his wife was pleased to flatter those people, it was nothing to him.

The three ministers of the three parishes of Apple Downs, who were present on the evening just noticed, were especially requested to favor Mrs. Cushing with their presence again on the third evening following; when they would meet with numerous members of their respective flock not among the first company.

Happily, Ralph was well and in good order for the second occasion; happily for him, as he would have missed more the simpler entertainment of the simpler folk, than he had missed that which was more fulsome, and on the whole, more brainless. There were staunch, sensible tradesmen in Apple Downs, and farmers of the same type on the broad, rich lands around ; men who fought sturdily the battle of life, and who thought while they fought, and who read and pondered the thoughts of other men. There were active, conscientious housewives, and well-trained young men and maidens, full of inherited good sense and native good manners. Of these the majority were well to do, and some were poor. They were growing accustomed to these entertainments,— for every year there was something of the kind,— and the first strangeness was so far wearing off, that some who could not be persuaded to come at first, were now throwing off their awkwardness, the timidity being exchanged not for boldness, — *that* were impossible in the presence of the Cushings, — but for a higher tone of self-respect, and a confidence in the sincere good-will of their entertainers. Thus, of all those invited, there were missing only the widow Rhoda Bailey and her two daughters. Little Rosa would have been glad to be of the number, but her mother and sister Amelia could see no propriety in accepting attentions that they could not possibly return. So little Rose found it quite essential to be resigned, and the more so that she had no acknowledged friend for escort. But Rose had learned the happiness of making others happy, and found her heart always more glad in listening to her mother's expressed judgment, than in advancing her own. " Why should I trouble mother," she would say, " with opposing my wish to her judgment? Ten to one her judgment is always really the best. And even if it be otherwise, it is far happier for me to make what remains of her life smooth and peaceful, than to have my own way." After all, Rose's " own way " was exactly what she was continually doing, viz., to contribute by every possible means to her loved mother's happiness.

The three ministers were there to a man.

There was Reverend Frank Clearwater, with large, serious blue eyes, and quick, bright, manly speech. He was accompanied by his friend, Professor Payn, whose inability to be present on the first evening was replaced by his ability to present himself on this occasion. If the exactness of his costume was somewhat fastidious, it after all did not assort ill with his well-made figure and his regular features. These last only wanted the play of a less conscious manner, and a freer smile to make them fine. Then there was the Reverend A. W. Hidden, with countenance of mildly benevolent cast. It was understood that the letters A. W. stood for *Amaniah Wiseman;* but, as Mr. Hidden was not himself partial to the name Amaniah, he invariably wrote himself A. Wiseman Hidden,—a name that was, on the whole, more suggestive to his parishioners and his immediate neighbors than to him. And then the cheery, stately, slightly pompous, very gentle Pastor Laidley, of the Scottish kirk. A favorite maxim with this good man ran somewhat thus: "Contentment and accuracy insure happiness." And, as he could never be otherwise than profound, (even his simplicity seemed profoundly simple), it followed that in personifying his own maxim, he became profoundly content and profoundly accurate. He was also profoundly original, — but that was not his fault, — and the gift was well carried and used only for good. When he was entreated that his maxim was a worldly one, conveying no ray of evangelical truth, he would say, — every syllable clarified with broad Scottish brogue, — " So also is the word 'Thou shalt love thy neighbor as thyself,' if it be left to the world's usage." He would then amplify much as follows: " The grace of the Lord brings contentment, and the truth of the Lord begets accuracy. And the fulness of the Lord's grace and truth is fulness of joy indeed."

These three good men were all beloved in their measure ; and it was good for them and for their respective churches to be thus thrown together, and thus once more reminded that they were all brethren, redeemed by one Saviour, fed by one Shepherd, owned by one Lord. The company numbered more than the first. Library, drawing-room, and spacious hall were as full as was comfortable, and in the words of Patty Jenkins, then present, "all in a buzz." The parlors were not thrown open, and for two reasons, both of which seemed to Mr. Cushing very silly, — but then he never troubled himself about "those people." In the first place, Mrs. Cushing had an instinctive dread of doing anything that could seem like displaying her possessions to her neighbors who had less than she. And then, further, the library and drawing-room were comparatively so plain as to afford a better sense of ease and comfort to her guests. That her judgment was not at fault in this last particular was evinced in a remark of one of the number, Elder Marius Jones by name, to Farmer Black, in the presence of good Doctor Laidley, and reported by him afterward to his own and the hostess' " profound " amusement. The three were standing in the hall, taking their coffee, (Mr. Cushing had consented to entertain without wine on this evening). The conversation had turned upon church matters, and Elder Jones was expressing himself quite disturbed because of the perverse impossibility of managing one " social level " in this world for all who are Christ's " I tell you, *domine*," he said, addressing with much emphasis his reverend neighbor of the Scottish kirk, " the mount of Zion mourns when one brother can't meet another on the same footing in all respects. I dare say it's all right, socially considered. We're in the world, and there must be divisions of trade or occupation ; and there must be grades of education accordingly The poor man can't have what the rich man has ; and the manners of us ploughmen can't be every way agreeable to men of learning ; nor theirs ain't to us, as I know of. (I beg pardon, domine ; nothing personal). But it does seem strange, unaccountable, and somehow sorrowful, that where the Spirit of Christ is, His love shouldn't prevail over all these differences, and even wipe 'em out. They come nearer to it *here* than any place, maybe," he said lowering his voice, and addressing Mr. Black especially. " Now these carpets ain't such as man is afraid to step on ; and, if I can't find a spittoon anywhere 'round, it isn't so much matter for one evening, so long as the chairs are stout enough to sit on. I told my domine the other day that if the convention of churches was to be in New York this year I wouldn't go. Not that I don't love the churches down there, (and Christ's people, be they rich or poor, love one another). I told him, not a doubt but that I would be well treated. I believe that on the whole the love of the Master rules in the churches, bad as things look sometimes. But if I was to go down there, likely as not I should be quartered with some rich family where I couldn't spit if I wanted to ; and though they wouldn't for the world hurt my feelings, I should be all the time afraid of offending theirs. On the whole, Pastor Laidley, these ministers of the Gospel — the real ones I mean are about the only learned folks that an unlearned brother can feel at home with. And these Cushings " — his voice fell nearly to a whisper again as he touched Farmer Black on the shoulder — " these Cushings are about the only *rich* ones where a poor man can feel sure he isn't in the way. Who doesn't like Mister Ralph ? And Miss Rebekah — ain't her words like apples of gold ?

" But what is the explanation of all this, that I believe is right in the main, because in the main necessary; and that yet seems somehow all wrong ? "

Farmer Black thought that social grades and distinctions, such as Elder Jones referred to, evidently ordained of God as suited to our present human estate ; and that, so long as the church on earth is made up of human beings, its members are members also of the great human family, and as such have certain social conditions to fill; having thus, perhaps, all the better opportunity to manifest the Spirit of Christ toward one another. To be sure, there is failure in man; but, as far as God's ordination is concerned, it is better for us to adorn it than to improve upon it.

"Ah!" said Doctor Laidley, "there you made an excellent point. In spirit and in truth God's dear children are all one in Christ Jesus; no barbarian and Grecian distinctions here. But under present conditions the practical and literal "all things common" seems contrary to the divine economy. Such a social system, when demanded by the peculiar conditions of the primary Jewish flock, was imprompted and inaugurated by the Divine Spirit in the church. It would be quite unsuited to ordinary times and conditions. Hence we find nothing of the kind transpiring in the Pauline churches, nor suggested in any of the apostolic letters. There is something higher and larger shown to us, — 'let the brother of low degree rejoice in that he is exalted, but the rich in that he is made low.' God desires to work in us absolutely after such searching and unworldly precepts as, ' Let all your things be done with love.' ' That ye love one another.' ' It is more blessed to give than to receive.' ' Remember the poor.' ' Honor to whom honor is due.' ' Above a servant; a brother beloved ' — hand in hand with ' Servants obey your masters . . . . pleasing them well in all things.' It is one chief glory of the Gospel," he continued, " that it revolutionizes society not by models and formulas but by the living energy of divine principles. This is manifest in looking over the social progress of evangelized nations. It is in a way not to please man but to glorify God. We see everywhere among the foremost results of a received Gospel the elevation of the masses; not in a way to confound, but to define and dignify, social distinctions; because in the earthly state, if not in the heavenly, these are for the best welfare of all. It would be impugning the wisdom of God to assume that the entrance of His truth should unhumanize humanity. Neighbor Black made an excellent point there: we best adorn God's ordination when we accept it as it stands. Albeit, as regards love, there is failure in us. We are called, as Christians, to adorn the doctrine of God our Saviour, *in all things.*"

Before good Doctor Laidley had reached the end of these remarks, which seemed directly the fruit of Mr. Black's happy sentiment, he found himself the oracle of quite an audience, for a number of interested listeners had gathered about him. One of these thought the reverend speaker was possibly right, but remembered that the only "peculiar condition" mentioned of the church in Jerusalem was that the whole multitude "were of one heart and of one soul."

Elder Jones, listening first to himself and then to the reverend doctor, had forgotten to drink his coffee, and returned now to that fleshly aliment. But finding it quite cold, he put down his cup with mild emphasis, exclaiming, "Hem!

If there's anything I *do* despise, it is any kind of cold victuals ! "

. . . . . .

It must have been at about the time this conversation occurred, that another scene was transpiring in the library. There was a group of four standing near one of the windows, — Rebekah, Ralph, and Professor Payne ; and between these two gentlemen, a kindly, motherly quakeress, who was informing them with some details of household science. This discourse was interesting to the Professor, because he was specifically an economist ; it was interesting to Ralph and Rebekah, because they loved every phase of Christian domestic life ; and it was interesting to all alike because of the rare simplicity of gesture, and diction, and sentiment that adorned the garb of gray. " You all believe," she said, " and thee knows, Rebekah, that the work in hand is always best done when the heart is toward God in it. But, after all, one can't make good bread, nor a good washing and ironing, unless one *learns how.* It is just so with all those qualities and habits that go to make up character, and that find both their nursery and their supreme dominion in household life. Neatness, order, punctuality, — all these have to be *learned ;* and if not acquired by our childhood's training, they must be *studied afterward.* We are not fit to enter any responsible position till we have learned lessons that give fitness for it."

A deal more the quiet woman in gray had already said; and she would have added more beside, had not Professor Payne at that moment plunged himself against an alabaster flower-stand, on which was a light vase filled with day-lilies and salvias ; thereby precipitating the vase to the floor, — his own self-possession going topsy-turvy with it. The poor man was in the depths of embarrassment, from which Rebekah sought in vain to extricate him. "It is of no consequence, Mr. Payne, I assure you ; not the slightest. See, the vase is not broken, and the

white and scarlet are in as fine contrast as
ever."

" Let me collect them and — replace them —
for you, Miss Cushing," stammered the frightened man. " I beg, I am sure I beg your pardon! mightily awkward!"

At this juncture his suffering reached its
climax, and his fair complexion the altitude of
blushes.

" Why Payne, my dear man, what's the matter?" said Mr. Clearwater, just then passing
that way.

"Oh! he is contrasting scarlet and white,"
said the mischievous Ralph, almost bursting
with the merriment he must restrain. " But,"
he added, with quick, true feeling seeking to
turn the shaft he had leveled, " I like the lilies
better alone, my sister and I never can agree
about flowers."

The quiet woman in gray drew him aside.
" Ralph Cushing," said she, " let a friend say
to thee thy tongue has a lesson to learn. It is

not in good training if thee can wantonly wound a neighbor with it — But I forget, — I am in thy house, not in mine. I must not beg thy pardon for reproving thee; but I do confess I might have waited a more just opportunity."

Ralph, with true manliness, was sincerely grateful, and too really contrite to take offence. " There couldn't be a better opportunity," he said.

But Professor Payne had been too absorbed in the calamity to overhear with any sharpness, and nothing had been noticed by him. Mr. Clearwater had helped in re-arranging the flowers, and in restoring the lost equanimity; and by the time Ralph was missed, he reappeared, having left his matronly friend in the care of one of her own first cousins; with whom, by virtue of their respective homes being separated by three and a half miles, she had not met for two full years.

" Ralph," said Rebekah, " the meteors have not been discussed yet. Mr. Clearwater is just telling me of a fine exhibition that he observed

7

a few nights ago. Now, with three learned
gentlemen at hand, I have a golden opportunity
for getting myself informed. The question I
raise is, *What are* meteors?"

"Must we all speak at once? I defer to my
superiors," said Ralph, bowing to the other two.

Mr. Clearwater in his turn deferred to his
learned friend the Professor; who in his turn
declared all subjects related to astronomy to be
quite out of his line, and suggested that Ralph
being fresh from scientific lectures, and given to
all sorts of reading, could doubtless best open
the subject.

Ralph was really disappointed at this; because, — wishing to know more on the subject
than he then did, — he had hoped that the Professor would say much that he could not. He,
however, took up in brief two or three of the
various theories; and thought either the lunar
theory or the planetary consistent enough with
known facts to explain the origin of meteoric
stones. But the class of meteors known in

strictness as *shooting stars*, was involved in more obscurity. There was, he thought, no authenticated instance of any one of these having fallen to the earth. Their physical character was, therefore, less well ascertained, but there was reason to suppose that they are of very light material.

" But how far are they from us ? " asked Rebekah. "And what brings them so suddenly within our vision, to be as suddenly gone ? Do they really *go out*, as a candle does, or do they only go away ? And what gives them such a light, and such a motion ? "

" In the case of aerolites," said Ralph, " from which are derived meteoric stones, the altitude, when seen, is certainly not very great, since they are then passing through our atmosphere. As to their disappearance, they both go out and go away ; since it seems that their light proceeds only from the intense heat to which they are brought in their tremendous passage through the resisting air, and on passing out of the air, they cease to grow. Before we can decide what gives them their motion, we must decide their origin."

"And the shooting stars?" asked Rebekah. "Is their light of a different source?"

"Many of them," said Ralph, "perhaps the majority, are seen at altitudes beyond the earth's atmosphere. They are, therefore, not simply incandescent because of atmospheric resistance, as is the case with meteoric stones. On the contrary, it seems well proved that they are self-luminous. They move also, with planetary velocity, as meteoric stones do not, and as a lunar projectile certainly could not. And this," said he, "is about the sum of what I am able to state; according to which there is about as much surmised as known. I dare say facts have accumulated since I turned my attention to the subject."

"Indeed, gentlemen," said Rebekah, when Ralph paused, "is all this only a little? And what does it mean? It is all very interesting, but, as you say, not all fact. And, in part at least, Ralph, you should explain your explanation. Do you really mean, for instance, that a planet of our system has at some time been destroyed ? "

" Oh, that is well known to everybody," said Ralph, with a twinkle toward Clearwater.

" Not so, Ralph," said Rebekah; " you are wrong for once, for I claim that 'everybody' includes me, and I did not know it."

" Ah, well ! " replied he, " I mean all except those mortals who are so devoted to Greek, and metaphysics, and needlework, that they overlook some other matters."

Mr. Clearwater suggested that the fact of all fallen aerolites being uniformly made up of four or five identical substances, would hardly comport with the idea of their planetary origin, since fragments of a broken planet could hardly be of such unvarying material. Ralph had not thought of this, and would be sorry to give up his pet theory.

"Then these showers that we encounter, especially in the months of August and November, are of shooting-stars, not aerolites ? " asked Rebekah.

" Oh, by all means not aerolites," said Ralph.

Professor Payne cited the *nebular theory*, which he remembered to have seen discussed somewhere, as accounting for shooting-stars. It seemed to him quite possible that the earth should encounter zones of nebulous matter, at certain given parts of its own orbitary course. Ralph advanced certain difficulties in the way of maintaining that theory, as, that there could hardly be zones of nebulæ passing within our system, yet only visible when so near the earth is to be disturbed by it. And the Professor remembered to have seen that some eminent scientist was so in despair of assigning this doubtful class of meteors to any cosmical origin, that he contented himself with considering the whole phenomena a freak of electricity."

Rebekah continued interested so long that she

was ashamed; and, coming to herself, she begged Ralph to attend to two forlorn persons at a little distance, who had no one to speak to them, at the same time excusing herself to the other gentlemen in order to look up a few of the guests whom she had not yet greeted.

———

" Mistress Cushing," said the quiet woman in gray as the company was breaking up, " I wish thee all sorts of prosperity in thy absence, and a speedy return to thy family and thy neighbors. Thee has a good escort in thy son, and he knows the way he should go."

CHAPTER VII.

THE DEPARTURE.

SWEETLY, softly, brightly, came the dawning of the day that was to witness the farewells and the departure. The house was early astir. Even Mr. Cushing had been slightly enthusiastic and melancholy by turns during the last few days, and this morning he was strangely impatient for the very last good and orderly breakfast that he could possibly expect to have for many months. What would become of the house he could not tell. He was perfectly sure that the travellers would not get off in season to make their first thirty

(104)

miles that day, and perfectly sure that everything at home would go to ruin after they had gone; and equally distressed with each of the two apprehensions. "was ever a Cushing the subject of such a complication of domestic agitations, or of necessity so tyrannical?"

Rebekah rallied him a little at this. "Why, papa, who is agitated? or what is there in agitation? Wait till you have had a cup of *my* coffee, made with my own hand — because Jane, in her hurry, knocked her edition off the stove — and your nerves will come so sweetly under it, that you will want me to make your coffee all winter. I expect you to be in admiration of my supervisory care of the house this winter, and *almost* reconciled to your unhappy lot, papa. And Jane has a superb omelet for you, — for *us*, shall I say? — and *such* muffins for all, but for 'Mistress Cushing' especially. The good creature!" — and Rebekah bit her lip to choke back the merriment at thinking, what she did not dare to say, — the thought that Jane had inevitably mingled a tear with every dish, — since the bright, perfect morning had, to her, been misty with weeping.

Just here Joan came to the library to say that breakfast was quite ready, and waiting; but mistress was receiving a caller in the drawing-room, and should she put the dishes by the fire again? — "for it wouldn't be no way right that mistress should have a cold breakfast *this* morning."

"It is not possible," said Rebekah, "that any one should detain Mrs. Cushing long at this hour. Who is it, Joan?"

"Oh, it's she that's Ethel's sweetheart?" said Joan with manifest indignation, but, in awe of Mr. Cushing's presence, afraid to say more.

"Ah, well, Joan, poor Faith is like the rest of us — not quite ready to let Mrs. Cushing go," — and Rebekah's voice shook slightly. But she controlled it instantly, and dismissed the hand-maid, saying, "Very well, Joan, we will come."

"Now, papa," she continued, "you like to

linger over your coffee, so we can easily overtake
you if you make a beginning without ceremony.
Come, *do*, papa " — taking his arm and leading
him off. There was something in Rebekah's
influence that always moulded her father more
or less, but this morning he was singularly pas-
sive, and contented himself with grumbling all
the way from the library to the breakfast-room.
Rebekah knew very well that the temper would
be smoother with the breakfast well begun, and
was determined with herself to have all "quite
right before mamma comes." Once seated, she
continued: " I am proud to pour for you a cup
of *my* coffee, papa. It is positively ambrosial.
Joan, don't you spill a drop ! "

" No, ma'am," said Joan, enjoying the episode
as much as she dared, and passing the coffee
with unruffled accuracy.

Meantime Faith Hopefield was unbosoming
some of her troubles to Mrs. Cushing, seeking a
stock of sympathy and counsel to fill up the
demand of the many months when the loved

face and voice would be absent. Faith had no
mother. She could remember her, and quite
distinctly, — her quiet, matronly face without a
wrinkle ; her uniform of gray without a spot;
her gentle "thee may, Faith," or "thee may
not, Faith," without ever a variation on key or
pitch; her sympathy often unspoken for very
depth; and her reprimand as often eloquent
with expressive silence. She remembered her
orderly and active industry, and many a practical lesson both of her life and precept. And
she remembered the parting, when she herself
was but nine years old. But the only of the
many last words that remained distinct in her
memory were those that she repeated to Mrs.
Cushing this morning: "The Heavenly Father
will have a special care for thee, Faith dear,
when thee is orphaned." And she felt herself
still orphaned, although for some years under
the supervision of a stepmother of unimpeach-
able rectitude.

"I sometimes think," she said, "that I have

taken those words presumptuously — not enough
in thankfulness and humility, and the right fear
of the good and loving God. I have been
father's only child, thee knows, and father never
could be stern with me. But he says it is a trial
to him that I should marry out of the Society,
and I am young yet to leave him."

"Ethelred would not wish you to marry
against your father's will," said Mrs. Cushing,
"neither should you. Much is sometimes
gained to all by patient waiting in such a case."

A few minutes later the fragrance of
Rebekah's coffee penetrated to the drawing-
room, and suggested to Faith that she must
have been very stupid not to bethink herself of
expedition without a hint so unmistakable.
She withdrew at once with her accustomed decorous modesty, but without apology, knowing
that Mrs. Cushing did not like apologies for un-
intentional oversight, — neither did she herself.

The coffee had done for Mr. Cushing's royal
temper what Rebekah's words could not do; so

that the breakfast-room was quite luminous when Mrs. Cushing entered. But, for an unusual occurrence, Ralph was missing.

" Joan, did you call Mr. Ralph ? "

"I went up to his room ma'am, but got no answer. I suppose maybe he's out setting Zed right, — Zed's quite out of his head, like, this morning, ma'am."

" There ! " said Mr. Cushing, "I knew very well something would turn up. Pretty well this! to pack you off with a crazy dinner! Joan, what is the matter with Zedekiah ? "

" Stumbles over everything, sir, and quite forgets what he comes for till he goes back without it."

At this juncture Joan grew so uncomfortable with repressed laughter that Mrs. Cushing relieved her by sending her for some hot muffins. And in fact Zed's state of mind had the effect to finish what the coffee had begun. Joan's manner of viewing the crisis was certainly happier than either Jane's or their master's.

"Mamma," said Rebekah, " papa's regard for you would have kept him waiting, but I was sure he ought not to wait longer. Haven't I made a good beginning, papa?"

" *Very.* You have made me quite comfortable, Rebekah." This was a great deal for Mr. Cushing to express, and both wife and daughter were by so much the happier for it.

"It is all just right, my dear," said Mrs. Cushing. "Poor Faith! Did you know I have had a call from Faith Hopefield? It pleased me very much that she should come to repeat the farewell."

" Was that all she came for, mamma?"

" No, dear, not all. You know she has always something to tell me."

Here Ralph entered, all aglow with the life of the fresh morning, his hands full of flowers, and his heart full of manly sympathy for every living thing. His words fairly tumbled over one another in description of his walk, and in explanation and apology for his tardiness.

"Oh, my *ready* Ralph," said Mr. Cushing, "good for an apology is good for nothing else. So says Doctor Johnson, and he must be right. At least the time was when he *must* be right."

"*Early* Ralph, *punctual* Ralph," said his mother, "the exception proves the rule. We must all excuse your '*malgre*,' even the apology."

" *Good* Ralph," said Rebekah, " come quickly, do, and taste *my* coffee, — *mine*, Ralph, a grand success just for once."

Ralph found himself quite overwhelmed with epithets. " *Ready, early, punctual, good-for-nothing, good*," said he slowly. Then laughing back to the first glow. " Good people, all, I have a story to spice our breakfast with. But first, now, *good* Rebekah, and '*quickly, do*' taste of my flowers. I could hardly make up my mind to bring you a white japonica this morning. But seeing you will prefer them, and wishing to do just the right thing, I *have* brought one."

Rebekah knew, but the others did not, why

when he begau speaking of the japonica both eye and voice softened a little.

"That is so good of you, Ralph."

"But," he continued, "I am not going to give it to you in all its own lone blankness. There! with a fuchsia on one side and two or three sprigs of heliotrope we shall get both ardor and fragrance. That will do," he added, as he placed them by her on the table. "And mamma, here are some superb roses."

"Oh, come to your muffins, Ralph," interrupted his father. "What is all this fuss about flowers? One would think human flesh could breakfast on nectar!"

"Yes, sir; yes, sir!" said Ralph, with a sudden departure of both animation and appetite.

Mrs. Cushing said something in joyous appreciation of the roses; while Rebekah, unwilling that the effect of the last remark should remain, sent around Ralph's coffee, and continued, —

"Metaphysician? poet? What shall we call you, Ralph dear? I insist that japonicas are not

8

soulless; not even inexpressive. They are *reticent;* they do not give out their best self to all alike. But interrogate them rightly and you cannot want a better acquaintance. Oh! I like them. I *like* them. I *do like* them!" And she took the japonica from the other flowers only for one instant. Then quickly placing all together again she added, "But I like fuchsias and heliotropes extremely. And really there could not be a more lovely combination than this, with just the one leaf of deep, deep green. I shall keep these until you come again, dear brother." But here her voice shook a little. She could not touch upon that.

"It is the strength and lustre of its own abiding green," said Ralph, "that redeems it, and sustains your argument."

"*Some* 'good in everything,'" murmured Mr. Cushing, with Shakespeare to back him. As Ralph had really fallen to work and was partaking in good earnest of tangible substantial nourishment, his father softened into so much of substantial praise. " But what about Zed? Have you seen him, Ralph ? "

" Why yes, sir, I have seen him. Nothing *about* him that I know of."

" Joan says he is quite topsy-turvy this morning." Poor Joan wished there were more muffins wanted.

" Oh! well, yes," said Ralph, " he was in a deal of trouble because he could not remember whether you had said corn or oats for the horse to-day."

" And what did you say ? "

" I told him that I knew nothing about it. I never knew you to have any choice for a single occasion ; and I supposed *oats.*"

" There ! " said Mr. Cushing, " You will be two smart men to take care of yourselves and an invalid ! It will be a wonder if you get started, and a greater wonder if you ever get back. I said *corn.* I should like to see Zedekiah hold Philip straight with oats in him such a morning as this, when he can't hold himself right side up."

This was too much for Joan, who darted out of the room almost choked with laughter, in which state she appeared in the kitchen, to the great scandal of Jane and Margaret.

"Oh, now father," said Ralph quietly, "you know there is no horse steadier under a firm rein than Philip. Hasn't Zed driven him for three years? And we all know him through and through. I am sorry I blundered counter to your wish, if blunder it was. But, soberly, do you really care so very much?"

"I don't care for the mere *fact* of the blunder, since there was no disregard. I *do* apprehend the *effect*."

But, as nobody else did, there was a brief pause; when Ralph continued,—

"Ethel seems in a woful way, too, this morning."

"What has Ethel to trouble him?" asked Rebekah. "I thought no one had a more quiet mind or more glowing prospects than he."

"I don't know what," said Ralph. "I told

him that you would give him news of us so often that he could hardly miss us. He said it was a grief to have us go, but that was not all."

" You have not given us your story, Ralph " said his mother, thinking it best to turn the current another way.

" Ah! I forgot," said Ralph, who by this time could eat no more. " I forgot for the moment; you have all kept me so busy. The story is not very long; only this: I met Professor Payne and Mr. Clearwater at the gate. They kindly took their morning walk this way in order to wish us a pleasant journey, and also to say that in the storm of night before last the turnpike near Evans' Ridge was very badly washed, and the bridge so broken that there is no passing. We must make the first fifteen miles either by Eagle Dell or that unpleasant Glenville road."

" *There!* " said Mr. Cushing, " I knew something would happen, — something would go wrong at the start. You will have to drive at least twenty miles to make fifteen, by either

of the side roads, — such narrow turnouts, — and
with oats, too ! "

" My dear husband," interposed the mother,
" let us look at it as it is for one moment. I
would not think of the Glenville road. It is
both rough and unpretty. But the way by
Eagle Dell is really very good, and through a
charming country. And since Zed is reliable,
and Philip is easily managed, and *the oats have
been eaten*, shall we not accept things as they
are ? For my part, I am very glad to go by
Eagle Dell. That was very kind, though, of
those two good gentlemen."

" Yes, *very*," said Mr. Cushing, who had a
high appreciation of neighborly courtesy. " But,
Mrs. Cushing, I know more about oats, and
horses, and these country roads than you do.
Now," he added, suddenly softening, and passing into his most courtly manner, " what is
to be done next ? "

" We are all ready, I think," said Mrs. Cushing. " The trunks are locked, ready for the

express; and our smaller luggage is easily gathered up. So we have quite time to read."

Mr. Cushing almost said *pshaw!* But he
knew that nothing would more surely or deeply
wound the wife he so fully respected, and whom,
somewhere in his heart, he really loved.

" Will you join us this morning ? " she asked.

" Yes. It is your last morning. . Yes, I will
come."

.   .   .   .

Ten o'clock found the last preparations com-
pleted ; all the kisses pressed, all the farewells
said.   Mr. Cushing not only allowed his wife to
kiss him, — he actually kissed her, warmly,
strongly, tenderly, *once*, — *twice ;* very much as
he had kissed her in days well remembered
twenty-five years ago. The sweet impress of
this new embrace sank down, down, into her
hungry, weary heart; and never, never faded
out of it.

The carriage was at the door. The servants
all stood near. Even Joan showed signs of

weeping. Penn and Philip looked well. So did Zed. The Eagle Dell road was decided upon, and there were no signs of anything wrong anywhere. Mr. Cushing took Ralph by the hand. "You will make good progress, I have no doubt, during these absent months. Write freely. And Ralph," he said kindly, "put a flower in your letters here and there, to Rebekah, if not to me."

Ralph knew that he must not seem to notice the implied retraction of what had been less gently said before. "Never fear, sir," he answered, "I shall write, and I dare say I shall study."

The seats were taken. "Ready, sir?" said the impatient Zed.

Ralph excused the fellow, but took no notice. He drew Rebekah towards him that he might speak in her ear softly; "I say, darling sister,— it is of more value that you pray than that you write. So, while you write, pray. And, *mind*, don't keep the house so well that papa will not want us back again."

"Dear, naughty boy!" said his sister, with a pat more loving than resentful, and that made his cheek tingle.

The signal was given, and the carriage rolled away.

. . . . ,

The reading of that morning had been from two of the evangelists, and there was a single verse from each that fixed itself in Mr. Cushing's mind. He could not put the words away. The first: "Blessed are the pure in heart, for they shall see God." The other: "He that is of God heareth God's words, ye therefore hear them not because ye are not of God." The first searching him through as with a scorching heat. And the other — what could it mean?

CHAPTER VIII.

COUSIN CECILIA'S WELCOME.

T is not at all necessary to our story that
we follow the travellers through all the
detail of their daily route. Devoting
very few words to it, therefore, we will
at once join them where they were first introduced to us after the broken axletree put
Ralph's ingenuity to the test and sent them on
their slow way to Mariondale. From the very
first, their chosen mode of travel proved of great
benefit to the invalid, who enjoyed more than

she anticipated; more, indeed, than Ralph had ever seen her enjoy before. As he expressed it when writing to Rebekah, " her enjoyment took on a freshness really youthful; throwing her habitual serenity, that must ever prevail, into contrast all the sweeter." Their progress of from twenty-five to thirty miles a day, with but one or two interruptions from rain, brought them to Ohio and their friends on the *Scioto* in little more than two weeks. Here they passed only two days, as the weather was growing sensibly cooler, and the days shorter. Thence their route lay nearly due South; and, crossing the *Ohio* River at ——, they proceeded still Southward, and a little Westward, through the rich, lovely country of " Old Kentucky," the oldest of the new States, till they entered glowing, lavish, delightful Tennessee.

At the time we left them on the road near Mariondale, they were a day or more south-west from Nashville, not far from the east bank of the *Tennessee* River. We now take up our narrative from that point.

"Mother," said Ralph, as they approached the village where lights had been for some time visible, "of course the Stanleys do not know at all when to expect us; neither the day nor the hour."

"Not the day, nor yet the hour," replied his mother. "True. But the late hour will not surprise them. You know I wrote from Dulwich that we like to drive in the moonlight, and might arrive at any odd hour. I am bearing this adventure remarkably well — even enjoying it. Your contrivance in lieu of saddle is a grand success, and the evening is so warm and perfect! It is wonderful how my strength has increased since leaving home, notwithstanding a shade of homesickness here and there. How dismal if this had occurred of a dark evening!"

"But we wouldn't have been driving of a dark evening, you know," suggested Ralph, adding, "Can you be sure of the house? You have not been here for a very, *very* long time, if your last visit was, as you say, when I was a *little* boy! How little was I then?"

"The average size of a four-year-old Yan-kee," said his mother tartly. "That was not so very long ago, Ralph."

"I dare say not," said he, laughing, "but I can remember events later than that, which seem dimly far off. I do assure you that the hair on my temples is sprinkled with gray. I pulled out two hairs, this morning, as silvery as any old man's. This pursuit of law is bringing me rapidly to a peaceful old age."

There was a dry bitterness in the tone with which Ralph uttered these words. They were his first allusion to the unloved subject of his new studies since the journey began. Their conversations, their books, their interchanged delight in the ever-changing scenery, had all tended to keep the theme out of mind, or to repress it. The remark that had now escaped him was half at unawares; and his own quick manner in changing the subject forbade any response. "Cousin Cecilia may not be unpre-pared for the odd *hour* of our arrival," he said, "but she is certainly unprepared for the odd *manner* of it. Were we only with saddle and pillion, on one horse, the farce would be complete."

But Mrs. Cushing thought the scene very complete as it was, since she was so uniquely mounted, and with a footman so very knightly. She might even be a queen.

"Oh yes, you might well have been a queen!" said Ralph.

Continuing their conversation, they approached the Stanley homestead almost before they were aware. On the outskirts of the village it stood, approached by a carriage-way embowered with magnolia and linden trees, and sweet with night-blooming jasmine. Mrs. Stanley was a lady of three or four and forty, and now for several years a widow. Surrounded with every good thing that wealth, joined with correct taste, could give, at peace with all the world, and full of energy for the duties of life. She devoted herself ardently to the training and happiness of her children, to the order and prosperity of the estate, and to the oversight and well-being of her tenants. With all this she sought, not in vain, for opportunity to reach, and in some way to bless, her neighbors near at hand and those far off. She had strong affections and disaffections. Her chief earthly joy and pride lay in her children, in whose moral and intellectual growth she was greatly and rightly absorbed. The oldest, Grace, then on a visit to an uncle in San Francisco, was seventeen. Then there were Mary, and Janie, and Frank, Janie being the youngest. The ages of these three children, physically beautiful (which they did not know), and mentally bright (which they found out for themselves), were respectively twelve, and ten, and seven.

It was half-past nine when the travellers approached the house. Ralph intended, by all means, to lift his mother down near the verandah, and then quietly lead the horses into the shadow of the shrubbery, after which they would shake off some of the dust and appear in very quiet garb at the door, two tired pilgrims soliciting entrance. He would not, 'for the world,' have his mother seen mounted in that fashion, and would only disclose their adventure after the first salutations were over. But what if the house-dog should bark! That would quite spoil their plan. Or if they should meet any of the servants, it would be so provoking!

No. The dog did not bark. He was soundly asleep under the library table. Mrs. Stanley was sitting near with some needle-work. Mary was occupied likewise, and Franky was yawning over *history*, which he disliked, and always put off till the other lessons were learned.

"It is past your bed-time, Franky," said his mother. "You are slow this evening. Mother thinks you have studied long enough. You shall get up early to-morrow, and, after a glass of milk, you can study awhile before breakfast."

Franky was ambitious, but he did not ask "Why mayn't I finish now?" but said only,

"Yes, mamma," and, closing the book, he added with the air of a philosopher, "I suppose I would learn this old history quicker when I am not so sleepy."

"*Old* history?" said Mary, "why, I thought you were studying modern history."

"You know what I mean, Mary," piped the little fellow. "It's *bothersome!* I can *learn* it, but I can't *like* it. But you don't think modern history is *young* history, do you? I'm sure it's old enough, all of it that I ever heard of. And I guess I am in the most ancient part of the modern, now, — away back in the rosy wars of York and Lancaster. The idea of such hateful people being named for white and red roses!"

"Oh, Franky! modern history begins long before that,— *ages* before," said Mary, looking very wise, and laughing because she was trying to look grave.

"Well," said Master Frank, "I should think it had *better* be called ' old history,' then, at that rate. Then we shall have Ancient, Old, Modern,

and *Recent*, that will be *young*, will it not? You
must write a history on my plan, Mary, when
you are grown up."

" If you want ancient history, you had better
read the Chinese," said Mary.

"Oh, now, the Greek is as old, I *bet* you,"
said Frank, " and a great deal nicer. But the
Roman, *the Roman* for me! Hurrah! I'm going
to bed."

" Franky," said his mother gently, "I don't
like you to say ' bet ' and ' I'll bet you.' There
is neither good feeling nor good taste in
that."

" All the boys do say so, mamma," said Frank,
a little irritated. "But I'll not say it, mamma;
I'll not," he added ardently, as he met her patient look.

At this moment Philip of Macedon neighed
long and loud, close to the house, and *again*,
even louder.

" What is that?" exclaimed all at once.

"I *bet* they've come," cried Frank. "Oh,

mamma, I didn't mean to! What *can* I say?
I'm *sure* they've come!"

And at this same moment poor Ralph was saying, "Oh, Philip! Why didn't you wait another
minute? just *one minute!* Now, *now* mamma!
There! You are safely down, and like a feather.
I do believe it is the smell of these jasmines
that makes Philip so provoking. They nearly
intoxicate me. Now they are tied, — the
horses I mean. Come mamma. What a grand
old house, — but *what* an arrival!"

Mrs. Stanley had checked Frank's impulse to
rush to the door. "No, my son," she said.
" We will not answer such an equestrian summons. They would not wish it. No doubt the
driver will ring presently; if indeed that *was*
one of Mr. Cushing's perfect arrivals.''

Ralph, — " the driver " — was so much in admiration of the ponderous old-fashioned knocker
that hung brightly polished where it had hung

for sixty years, that he did not look further for a possible bell-knob, and his rather faint knock failed to arouse black Richard who was nodding in the dining-room. Franky ran "to punch him up," as he called it, and by that time Ralph's better sense enabled him to pull the bell. "Richard, *hurry!*" said Frank, out of breath, "I'm sure it is some one I want to see very much."

"Beg pardon, Mas'r Frank," said Richard, rubbing his eyes open. "Yes, sir, right away."

In another moment the guests were shown to the reception room.

. . . .

"Dear Cousin Helen Cushing!" exclaimed Mrs. Stanley, entering with both hands extended. "How good, how *good* to see you! And after so long a time! I had thought I should be quick enough to meet you at the carriage. And Ralph, too, my cousin Ralph! I can hardly make it seem real,—so like a stranger, and yet not a stranger. I am so glad,—*so glad* to see you! These are my Mary, and my Frank. Do let us lead you to the library where we were sitting. It is a pleasanter room, and will give you the *home feeling* at once."

Of course this was not a connected speech. All were speaking together, in that pure flow of gladness and genial greeting that belongs ·to the meeting of friend with friend, and makes confusion harmony.

Mrs. Stanley was anxious that Richard should send Sam at once to escort Zed and the horses to the stables, and could hardly credit her ears as to the breaking down, and the manner of accomplishing the last two miles. And Zed sick, too! Then the absolute perfection of Mr. Cushing's carriage had belied itself! The naughty thought would come, but there was too much true feeling to allow it spoken.

Everything had to be told, from the day they left home. And Franky waited so long to hear, that the mocking-birds under his window did not wake him in the morning, and he got a bad mark in history.

When Ralph found himself alone in his room, that night he was not at all ready to sleep. The events of the journey from the beginning, just narrated in a general way for their cousins' benefit, crowded upon him more in detail, and seemed to him amazing in their sum and sequence. Not that there had been many of striking import in themselves considered. But the whole chain of daily progress and incident; the variety of pleasant trifling adventures without one mishap or hindrance until the very last; the smooth procession of each day's stage as planned ; and above all, the happy advance already made in his mother's condition ; all this filled him with wonder. Then the good news from home (they had found letters in Nashville two days back) seemed to render everything complete. In all, and in everything there was diversion, life, happiness; yet Ralph confessed, *felt*, that he was not happy. Miserable he certainly was not ; but he was not *at rest ;* and to him rest seemed the essential quality of happiness — the desideratum of existence — the prime condition toward complete being and efficient work. Then all those conversations with Rebekah passed through his mind. Those words, " You will never be at rest until you are sure of it, too," sounded strangely then as now. " They were naturally enough spoken," he thought; " spoken in response to my question if she was sure of the Godhead of Jesus. Yet I think I could not ask that question now. That is, I suppose I am sure of it, since I am sure I do not doubt it. But it cannot seem to me as it does to her. It is not ' *precious*,' as mother would say. I cannot think mere credence given to a dogma is what God esteems as faith. Even admitting that the One who ' upholds all things by the word of His power,' is the one who ' by Himself purged His people's sins,' how can I know that I am one of those ' purged ' ones ? Rebekah says this is not to be *gotten*, it is to be *received ;* or rather, she said that *He*, Himself, the Redeemer, is to be received. But I am sure He is not one of my acquaintances. And He never can be *one* till He is the *chief* one; I am equally sure of that."

Ralph had never thought it unmanly to bend the knees before God. He had always thought the refusal to do so unworthy of true manhood. But he was not always able to do it; either from the sore, sore sense, or that blank *want* of sense, that he had no heart in it; or, though the heart was in need of speaking, a strange feeling that he could not reach God. To such mental frames the believer in Jesus — the child crying 'Father' — need not yield; because the new and living way which God has opened is always open, and faith is more than feeling. The mind of God does not change concerning this.

But this evening Ralph's heart was too full for anything else than a kneeling and an utterance. He knelt. He made no record of what was said, and we make no inquiry. He had no vision, and arose much as he had knelt; with longing unrelieved. Yet he was not tempted to impugn God's compassion, nor to think that He did not listen. But those great questions concerning **the** forgiveness of Sins, life in Christ, and the possession of it, — fellowship with the risen Jesus; when would these be settled?

As he lay down, the words came to his mind — 'Unto you, therefore who believe, He is *precious.*' "I wonder," thought he, "I wonder what this believing is?"

Poor Ralph! He was always *thinking, thinking.*

CHAPTER IX.

EXT morning, at breakfast, there was naturally a great deal said, or said over again, about home and the journey. The visit in Ohio, and the progress through Kentucky, were especially discussed. Zed, left in Nashville, seemed to Mrs. Stanley suggestive as illustrating one difference between free service and bond service.

"When our servants are sick," she said, "we feel bound to take care of them. The comparison must not seem odious. I do not know whether our way be owing to the interest of

(138)

ownership, or to some other difference in the two cases."

Mrs. Cushing thought the matter of self-interest not necessarily a selfish one after all. Property in anything enhances interest, and rightly so. But viewed in the light of philanthropy, the cases should be exactly equal. They had remained with Zed a day, and then, finding he had been right in supposing that some old acquaintances were living in Nashville, and that they were quite glad to give him a room and take care of him, he had begged that he might not be a hindrance to their progress if Ralph preferred driving to waiting. The physician had thought he would not be severely sick, but might be unfit to proceed for several days. He had contracted fever and ague on the way, together with a cold from a severe wetting.

"It is quite a marvel," said Mrs. Stanley, "that you did not all get fever and ague driving so much in the evening, and in an open carriage. Did you not know it is a great exposure in some localities?"

" Yes," said Mrs. Cushing, "I confess we did know it. But, as Doctor Saywell had instructed us how to guard ourselves with quinine if there should be any such exposure, I felt quite persuaded that we were safe. The days have been so uncomfortable, and the nights so superb! I must exonerate Ralph."

"You are very good to exonerate me, mother," said Ralph, " but, after all, since you are in my care, I am responsible. Rebekah would not let me off so easily, — the good, prudent Rebekah! Really, mamma, I had thought that Rebekah's guardianship would enrich your way more than mine. But with her curacy you would not have been allowed these moonlight gambols; I am quite sure of that. As for Zed, he *would not* take the quinine."

" *Our* servants do as they are told," interposed Frank.

"Ah! But Zed was not 'told,' Franky," replied Ralph good-naturedly.

"Oh, Franky boy!" said his poor mother.

And then addressing the others, " You must excuse him, — I trust you will. He is too much with rough boys at school."

" Why! Was that rude, mamma?" asked Frank. "I said only what was exactly true. I didn't *feel* rude."

There was a laugh at this, and Frank felt quite restored.

. . . . . .

There had yet been no account of Ralph's plot for delaying their arrival by an appeal to the hospitality of the house by the way. Black Sam, with Ned (who was quite a smithy and general tinker), had been sent at an early hour with the two horses, to bring the broken-down carriage. Some allusion to this brought out the omitted episode.

" I thought," said Ralph, "that it would be safer for mother than so long a ride on horseback. And then it would have added so much to the adventure! Anything for adventure! I mean, of course, anything reasonable."

" But really!" exclaimed Mrs. Stanley, " the idea of spoiling us of the pleasure of receiving you just when and as you came! True, your thought for your mother was good. But she has not suffered; so I am at liberty to be very glad that you came on. You would have been well received at the white house, no doubt; indeed, more than well received. They are a very estimable, well-bred family. Great friends of Franky, too."

" Why, where was it, mamma?" asked Frank.

" From Cousin Ralph's description, the house must have been the Jamesons'."

" No? You don't say so! Oh, I wish you had gone there, Cousin Ralph. Fred Jameson is a *bully* fellow."

" Franky, that is not a word for you to use, my dear boy! Besides, if words mean anything, Frederick Jameson is not that. Can't you give your cousin a better portrait of him ? "

" Oh, I reckon I *might*, if I had some chalk and a blackboard," said the naughty Frank, with a shy look at his mother to see if he must beg pardon for his fun.

"Try what you can do with your tongue, Franky," said Ralph. "A word-portrait is sometimes very good."

"Fred Jameson is *Mr.* Jameson, properly," said Frank, drawing himself up on his friend's behalf. "But I remember him since he was seventeen, and so I have always called him 'Fred.' He is twenty-three now. He is tall enough, and handsome enough, but not remarkably tall nor remarkably handsome. He has brown hair, and no particular kind of eyes that I know of. Perhaps what you call *gray* eyes. Now is he *drawn* sufficiently, Cousin Ralph?"

"Why, yes," said Ralph pleasantly, "I think you have done all that the chalk could do, and more. But of other points, — *qualities, characteristics*, and so on. What makes you like him?"

"Oh, I don't know!" sighed Frank, "I can't help it!"

"There is something lovable about him," said Mrs. Stanley, "and something that commands respect. That is the long and short of it. He takes care of his mother and sister. His father was a small planter, but died involved, and most of the estate was sold. Frederick, with his younger brother and one servant, carries on what remains. He also has great fondness for carpentry and joinery-work, and fills up odd hours with that. The strange thing is, that with all this activity and practical ability, and with a deal of general reading, he is at once the most meditative and the most delightful character that one could well find, — nothing sombre about him, — nothing unmanly. Such a character could hardly be drawn in a book without perpetual inconsistencies. But there it is, a living fact."

"Quite a character, indeed!" exclaimed Mrs. Cushing.

"Yet no prodigy, I dare say," said Ralph. "As a rule prodigies are detestable."

"Oh, nothing detestable about it," said Frank, looking very red, first with anger, and then with shame that he had been angry. "But mamma has not told the best."

"What is the best?" asked Mrs. Cushing and Ralph together.

"He preaches," said Frank.

"He does what? *Preaches?*"

Mrs. Stanley laughed, and assured them that Frank had made no mistake. The young man had fair gifts, and a great love for Gospel work; and held a license to preach given him by some ministerial convention. He now often held religious services as he found opportunity, — sometimes in the open air.

"This is very interesting!" said Mrs. Cushing. "But he is very young. Do you feel sure it is all well-judged and stable?"

"Oh, no doubt of it whatever. He has been well tested now, and is occasionally called upon to supply some pulpit."

"It is quite evident that he is no upstart,"

said Mrs. Cushing. " But he is very young to be in such a work, and so much noticed. In general, one would be what we call 'spoiled,' under such circumstances."

" I think not," said Mrs. Stanley, " where there is a real work of God in the soul, and the individual is absorbed rather with God's glory in Redemption than with his own position or gifts. Frederick very well said, in one of his recent addresses, that religion is more than excitement or impulse, — more, even, than great emotions and purposes; more than regrets and aspirations. It is *thought*, — earnest thought, living thought, sober, divine; such thought as God gives; thought that has the mind of Christ. Hence, he said, if we would use terms correctly, as God always does use them, *religion* is more than *conversion*. Conversion is *a turning again* in the right direction; a turning toward God. Religion is a *binding again*; a binding of heart, thought, life *to* God, — that is, to Christ Jesus, by whose spirit we cry to the Father.* This

* E. g. compare John xiv. 6, with Galatians iv. ˉ

state, he said, is a new state, — the result of a new creation, a sovereign work. It is always thoughtful, for it has the mind of Christ. It is always active and self-possessed, for it has the love and the Spirit of Christ. The man who is filled with it seeks to bless and to comfort, to lift up and to save ; because, being himself saved, he has become debtor to all. And while in the world, he yet seeks to keep himself unspotted from it as responsible to the Lord whom the world still crucifies."

" I might repeat much more. His speaking is with singular clearness and vigor, and his expressions easily remembered."

" Do, then, give us some more, by all means," said Mrs. Cushing.

" I don't know about giving you a sermon for breakfast," said Mrs. Stanley, laughing.

" Oh, never fear !" said Ralph, " we shall eat our breakfast. I join mamma in asking for more."

Mrs. Stanley continued : " Of course I give

you the merest abstract. 'This binding to God,'
he said, ' is unlike any other bondage.   It is not
of earth, but of heaven.   It is the normal state
of the creature, and profoundly so of the redeemed creature.   It is the sweetest and most
absolute servitude, flowing out of adoption to
the now loved object of worship.   Every responsibility of the soul toward God is enhanced
by redemption, as truly as every relationship is
endeared.   The human life of Christ does not
derogate from, but interprets God's sovereignty.
If God be infinite, then His sovereignty is infinite.   And if all of God be absolute then His
sovereignty is so.   Him, therefore, the soul, willing or unwilling, is bound to serve.   And to
Him the willing soul is bound ; but by what
endearing bonds ! since He is reached by the
Way, the Truth and the Life, — the risen, living,
everlasting witness that sin has been put away.'

" And towards the close of the sermon were
these words : ' Religion then, dear friends, or
the state that the word indicates, is *thought,*

but it is thought in the mind of Christ; thought that lives outward, — that breathes and acts; having its life in and from the Lord of life, the Saviour.' "

Mrs. Stanley had given them quite a discourse; of which, indeed, none of them were weary. But Mary, seeing that Mrs. Cushing and Ralph were silent, ventured to say : —

" Mother can quote Frederick Jameson by the hour. I don't comprehend how she does it."

" Oh, not by the hour dear child," said her mother. " Frederick never speaks an hour. I confess to retaining what he says more readily than what I hear from some others."

" Indeed you have quite favored us," said, Mrs. Cushing sincerely.

Ralph thought the best of all was near the first; those words — ' Religion is more than great emotions and purposes. It is *thought;* living, sober, divine.' " Was not that well said, mother ? " he asked.

Mrs. Cushing hesitated, and then answered,

"Yes, as it was amplified afterward. It would not so well stand alone."

Ralph looked incredulous. He thought a proposition that could not stand alone hardly worthy of support. "Doubtless," he said, "you know more about it than I do."

Mrs. Stanley looked at him inquisitively, but said nothing.

The breakfast passed off pleasantly. Frank begged to be excused, that he might have a few minutes with the respected, disagreeable history before school. Little Janie crept around shyly to Ralph, and put her hand in his, regarding him with a very wondering pair of large hazel eyes. It did not take long to make his acquaintance; and, her lessons being with her mother, she begged for a little time to lead cousin Ralph to see her rabbits and other pets. This being granted, the two ladies withdrew to the library.

The library was so called rather by courtesy than otherwise, and because the word *sitting room* was not in vogue with the Stanleys. It was light and spacious; and, having windows on sou h and east, was by far the pleasanter family room for winter than either of the parlors which were lighted the one from the north and east, the other from the north; the house facing east. One side only of this winter habitat was devoted to book-shelves, which, in keeping with the furniture, were of oak. One window, *only* one, was filled with flowering plants. Mrs. Stanley said that she had no fancy for living either in bower or booth; that she must have unobstructed daylight on at least one side, and a firm sense of something solidly architectural about her. This was quite essential, she thought, to anything like a due appreciation of our advantages as creatures of a civilized age. But against the book-shelves was trained a magnificent English ivy of most luxuriant growth, that went branching upward and outward in such provoking profusion that it taxed all the ingenuity of the combined family to keep it so trained as to allow free access to the books.   These looked all the more attractive and good for something under the bright shade of the branching green.   And, to the credit of the family be it said, they were not only well kept, but they were well read also.   Their contents often afforded themes for conversation that lasted for days, and sent the children exploring up and down the shelves to get some question answered.   A small library, if well selected and intelligently used, is one of the greatest of earthly goods.   So thought Mrs. Stanley, and so the children were early learning.   The only inmates of the room who never read were Rex the spaniel, and Jack the canary.   But Rex had the appearance of thinking a great deal; and Jack was happy with his observations and his song.

Ralph was delighted to be led by Janie, who, in her turn was very proud to lead Cousin Ralph.   She proved a very entertaining escort; her prattle being rather beyond her years, without the least self-consciousness or affectation,—

the simple outflow of well-trained feelings in a child of ardent temperament and bright intelligence. And Ralph proved a good listener; interested and responsive. This was what made him so delightful a companion to all, old and young alike. He not only knew how to talk, but he knew how to listen. The one is as essential as the other to good companionship, and even to the discharge of common courtesy. It was his attentiveness and his suggestive responses that held Janie to him this morning, though the charm did not define itself to her notice and she probably could not have explained it to herself. Before they reached the rabbits they were turned aside in two or three directions by different objects, of interest to both. Susan's boy Ben, — the blackest boy that Ralph had ever seen, — was feeding them with some dry crusts and some clover. There were two white ones, and two black with white paws.

"Aren't they pretty, Cousin Ralph?" said Janie. "And so tame! and so clean! and so

soft!   And oh, Cousin Ralph, they are so *knowing!* They know Ben from me right away."

Ralph had to laugh a little at this. "Yes,
Janie," he said, "they are beauties, and I dare
say they know a great deal. But there is a
great difference between you and Ben."

"Ben," said Janie thoughtfully, "this black
one is exactly as black as you. But then you
haven't white paws, Ben, so you are the blackest."

"Oh, now, Miss Janie," chuckled Ben, "that's
too good! But Miss Janie is part way mistaken.
I'se got big whites to my eyes, and plenty of
white teeth. I reckon him and me are about
even." Here Ben fell into hilarious merriment
that showed his white teeth to enormous advantage. Janie went on about the rabbits.

"They are so pretty when feeding, Cousin
Ralph! They *feed*, but *we eat*. I never thought
of that. What makes the difference? Why
don't we feed?"

Ralph smiled. "Some persons do, Janie," he
said.

" How ? Tell me, please, Cousin Ralph. What is the difference ? "

Ralph laughed again. " Eating," he said, " admits of conversation ; feeding does not. As the rabbits have no occasion to converse, they commit no breach of good manners in devoting their whole attention to their food."

" Then a man who forgets everything while he eats, just to attend to that, is feeding. Is that what you mean, Cousin Ralph ? "

" It is as well to say so," said Ralph. " At all events, it would be good for him to mend his ways."

Janie was stroking a rabbit with each hand. " How pink their ears are," she said. " And they are always moving them. There must be some nice arrangement, that they can put them forward or backward as they choose. How strange that they should like crusts and clover, and eat one as well as the other ! We could eat the crusts very well, but I don't think we could eat the clover. I suppose it must be that it tastes different to them."

"In general we dislike what is not suited to us," said Ralph.

"But we do eat some green things," replied Janie. "In the spring we eat watercresses."

"Yes; but spring clover you could not persuade yourself to eat if you tried."

"But is it only that one tastes good and the other does not?" asked Janie.

"No," said Ralph. "Our taste most often determines our selection. But our experience would teach us to reject the clover, if we ate it once."

This was a little beyond Janie, who looked puzzled. Ralph, seeing this, added, kindly, "You must get your mamma to give you some first lessons in physiology, where you will find some of your perplexities cleared up."

"I will," said Janie, "for I want to understand these things. Physi — what did you say, Cousin Ralph?"

"Physi — ology," said Ralph, slowly, as they walked away.

.   .   .   .

Janie was sure the half-hour was not up; her mother had given her half an hour. And as Ralph's watch declared that they had yet ten minutes the child must needs show him where the oriole's nest hung. It had been inhabited by a large family this year; all now fledged, and grown, and flown away. Two were brighter than the others. There it hung on the twig of a quince-bush; a strange place for an oriole to build. There were others in the oak trees and the tallest lindens, but this one yearly built in this green spot.

"*This* one, or *some* one. How long do they live?" asked the child.

"Indeed I don't know, Janie. You must put me into ornithology."

"Ornithology! Cousin Ralph! You make long words. What is that?"

Ralph laughed. "The classification of birds," he said, "and their natural history is called ornithology."

"Well, I don't know what *classification* is,"

said Janie, looking funnily sober; "but I suppose natural history is the history of their natural lives. And that would tell us how long
they live. Are all birds called 'sparrows,'
Cousin Ralph?"

"Why no, Janie," said Ralph, "no more than
they are all called orioles. What put that in
your head?"

"Oh, people speak so sometimes," said Janie.
"They say 'God feeds the sparrows.' And
Jesus says that our Heavenly Father does not
forget one of them. I always thought it meant
all birds."

"Yes, Janie, yes; it does mean all these,"
said Ralph quickly, astonished at the child and
ashamed of himself. "But," he added, "I
suppose Jesus spoke of them there as being
among the very sweetest birds, — so small that
two were sold for a farthing. Even the smallest
one not forgotten before God. By this we may
be sure He does not overlook the least of us."

"I thought so," said Janie.

"But, Janie, are you sure that God Himself feeds every one of these little birds?"

Janie looked up. The hazel eyes pierced him. His own quivered before their steadiness. They smote him; they held him. Unconsciously both stopped in their walk. Inquiry, perplexity, pain, all this was in those upturned eyes. Then she drew his hand that he might sit with her on the grass, and, putting her head on his knee, she burst into weeping.

"Why, Janie!" he said, "little Janie!" — and his own voice grew unsteady, — "how is this? I would not put the question just so, perhaps. I think we are both sure of it. But I don't know *how*, I am sure of it; and I thought you might help me."

The faith of a child, or a child-like faith, in the case of any one unaccustomed to sophistry, is alarmed and bewildered at the first hint of skepticism regarding anything divinely true and already received. Janie had never heard such a question raised before; and, being perfectly happy in her belief of all the words of Jesus, she was startled, — first into an unconscious dignity of bewildered feeling, and then into a revulsion of weeping. It is not in a child to speak soon again after such a commotion; and there were several minutes of silence, seeming longer to the distressed Ralph than to her.

"Janie, my poor little Janie, we must go," he said.

"No, Cousin Ralph, not yet. Mamma will excuse me. I didn't know I was going to cry. What strange questions you ask me! *Am* I sure, or *how* am I sure of something that Jesus says? I never thought of it before. He is the Lord, and knows all things. I am sure of everything He says because He says it."

To Ralph there seemed nothing weak in this unreasoning trust; only the quality of something greater than human, as if divinely imparted. The judgment of all men, learned and unlearned, places the authority of conscience above that of reason, and the moral nature over the intellectual. And of all moral qualities the highest is that of faith in God, — that quality which listens when God speaks. Ralph felt this, and that his own intellectual difficulties, which he sometimes fancied lustrous, were palling before this light, and discovering their own deformity. He had already shivered in the apprehension of having caused "one of these little ones" to stumble. And now the words that his mother had read on that last morning at home came to his mind; "He that is of God heareth God's words."

"This child hears the words of Christ and of God," he thought, "in a way that I do not; and. I do not find how to do it. 'He that believeth shall not make haste.' That *not making haste* certainly signifies a state of quietness, — a quietness that is not at all expressed by unconcern, but by *settledness — rest —* rest under the shadow of the Almighty. I have seen it in my mother; in Rebekah; and now here it is in this little

11

child. The least in the kingdom of heaven is greater than the sages."

. . . .

This time Janie thought the silence long. She said so, and they went in.

CHAPTER X.

FIRST LETTER FROM MARIONDALE.

TEN days passed away. Mrs. Cushing, either from the sudden change to complete inactivity, or from the fact that the journey had really been too much for her strength, and accomplished under more excitement than she had been conscious of, lost ground somewhat — to her own disappointment and Ralph's great disquietude. His increased anxiety on her account, and care of her, together with the daily walk or drive and the many attractions of the book-shelves, had kept him from getting very much absorbed in his own law-books. He said that he must give himself one week to get the home feeling on, and then go to work in earnest. The library, though much smaller than his father's, contained some books of a class that the latter was deficient in ; and Ralph's zeal to read everything of real excellence that he had never met with before was somewhat irrepressible.

It was early of a sunny afternoon. Ralph and his mother were in the east parlor, the short session of after-dinner lessons being in progress in the library. Mrs. Cushing was reclining on one of the sofas, and the conversation of the last quarter of an hour had given place to silence. Letters from Rebekah had enriched the morning. "Everything went well," she said. " Her mamma would rejoice to see how admirable her housekeeping was. Even her papa found no fault. Indeed he was singularly considerate, and pleased to be pleased with everything ; and her mamma would be really flattered to see how he watched for letters, and how how he devoured them, and discussed them, and made himself happy over every word of improvement on her part. They had just received their first letter from Mariondale, and had been much amused at the manner of the final arrival. Mr. Cushing had taken the account of the breaking down quite coolly for him ; saying he knew something would happen before they .got through, and thanking his stars that Philip did not kick up and dash them both out. Poor, dear, papa !" she continued. " He does not know how to thank any higher power or goodness higher than the stars. We are of course more together now than ever before; I am able to do more for him ; and he softens and expands wonderfully under the real trial of your absence; so that I am receiving much from him, and in ways quite new. I have never realized, until now, how far some of papa's ways that have been trying to me may have been owing to real infirmity of organization ; an affliction to himself. He is quite disposed to have his evenings prefaced with a drive, and filled out with some reading together, or with conversation on what we have seen or read; and often your letters afford fruitful theme for comment for days. I am satisfied that it is largely by force of that tremendous *will* of which he is possessed that he submits himself to the new order of things; he *will* make the best of your absence This keeps his best side always to the sunlight. But there is a love at work also. Deep down in his great soul, too long smothered by him and concealed from us, is an unselfish affection toward you, now exalted into a determination that you shall be allowed to receive all possible benefit and comfort in what, at our urgency, you have undertaken. Of all this he said very little; much less than I have said here; but in some way he makes me feel it, *see* it, continually. He speaks often of Ralph, and is evidently counting much on his future.

" Ethelred goes about, not gloomily, but like one broken down. He says he is not sick. I imagine there must be something not of the smoothest between him and Faith, or her family. The others of 'the Cushing retinue,' as Ralph calls these good creatures who make house-keeping tolerable, are moving in their smooth, beaten track; Joan beaming with every bit of intelligence from you, and Jane dissolving in tears. As for William and Margaret, so long as 'the bairns' are not sick, your absence is en-dured philosophically. *Zed*, poor fellow! They are all in lamentation over Zed's sickness, even Joan. But congratulations concerning your im-provement predominate.

"I miss, *miss* the after-breakfast readings, — the solace, the establishment, the renewal of thought and of soul-strength that we always found there. This is the time of day when your absence seems the hardest. But, oh mamma! how much I miss *you, — all the time!*"

This somewhat lengthy extract from Re-bekah's letter is given as being of interest after our recent acquaintance with the home at the Cushing mansion. It was this letter, chiefly, that had formed a text for the conversation between Ralph and his mother which had just lulled into silence. And, while the letter continued to occupy Mrs. Cushing's thoughts, Ralph, who had been reading the classics of human law all the morning, turned to a small book that he had spied out in the library as something strange or new to him, and had brought away to examine. *Thomas a Kempis.* He had, of course, a vague knowledge of him as a devout monk of the middle ages, who had left to the world or the church a book called " The Imitation of Christ." But his acquaintance further than this he had never made, and his book he had never seen. He sat now running his eye over the pages, held and led on by the dreamy, unfanciful, yet half-real dialogues between disciple and master. The quiet was interrupted, not disturbed, by the entrance of Mrs. Stanley. Lessons were over, and the already-arranged order of the afternoon was a drive of four miles to a neighboring plantation, where, in that courteous lack of all ceremony so peculiar to well-bred Southern life, they would pass an hour or two with Mrs. Stanley's valued friends, the Claytons.

Zed had turned up three days before, quite recovered; lavishly glad to be re-instated in office, and wofully ashamed of having been sick. Thus, the Cushings' carriage being provided with a new axletree, and the horses with their old driver, Mrs. Stanley was to be seated with them, and the children would follow on in the pony-carriage, which Frank was proud to drive. The drives around Mariondale never became wearisome, more especially as one rarely need return by the way one had driven out. Their way to-day lay through the village. There were two long, straight streets, very wide, running parallel to each other, lined on either side with two-story white houses, and bordered with two rows of magnificent trees, interlined by a third row, thus forming two complete archways of living green one mile long. Each street was like a copy of the other, with broad turf and smooth road-ways stretching out under the shade. These streets were intersected at right angles by two shorter, somewhat narrower ones, to which the warehouses and the trading were confined. The village was a sort of centre for the plantations for miles around, being the market for their ordinary purchases, and the point whence most of their produce was freighted to Nashville and the landings on the Tennessee river.

"How delightful!" exclaimed Mrs. Cushing, as they came upon the first long, green street. "How charming! I suppose, Cecilia, your antipathy to booth and bower doesn't allow you to enjoy this as you ought to. Oh, I say again, how charming! how delightful!"

Mrs. Stanley was overjoyed that her own dear Mariondale was so well appreciated, and protested that she enjoyed it none the less because preferring to live with a secure sense of cornice and panel about her. After driving the entire length of the two streets, admiring everything admirable, and duly criticising the odd interspersion of homely and elegant houses, they emerged into the rich, open country, and drove on, partly through groves and partly through cotton-fields, toward Clayton Hall.

Mrs. Clayton was more than glad to see them; and, embracing Mrs. Stanley with unaffected sweetness, received her two friends and guests with a royal ease and cordiality quite consistent with her claims as a descendant of Pocahontas. They were duly introduced to her daughter Maria, who had received her name certainly not by virtue of her maternal descent; but in accordance with a conceit of her father's that Grecian mythology and Athenian culture, either in name or aspect, should stamp his entire domain. In all other respects he was a reasonable and average gentleman. Miss Maria was pretty enough; but had the dark eyes and

the deviating nose — neither aquiline nor flat-
tened, but yet as far from the Grecian type as
possible, that at once betrayed her appellation a
standing misnomer, grim and graceless in its
abiding irony.   Her two brothers being that day
away from home, and Mr. Clayton not then in
the house, it devolved upon her to entertain
Ralph ; who, it must be said, found himself well
entertained.   There was something in Maria
Clayton's conversation fairer than the weather,
and larger than the space between North and
South.   Plantation life is not favorable to the
growth of gossip; and her charity, as well as
her good sense, was entirely averse to anything
savoring of sharp personalities or petty criticism.
(*Apropos:*   We see a deal of charity whose
good sense is not manifest ; and there are many
worldly-wise, good-sense people whose hearts
are too dry a soil for charity to grow in.
But the ideal of charity, as somewhere sketched
by Paul, is both sensitive and sensible.)

The mere fact that Maria Clayton had been

'educated at the North did not make her education any better; but it naturally gave a turn to
her introductory words with Ralph. She had
never been on the Hudson, and she asked from
him some description of the palisades and highlands; of West Point, and of his own home.
Her enthusiasm regarding all that is finest and
fairest in nature was as impartial as it was spon-
taneous and free. They fell into some discussion of the unhappy differences, nominally
political, but really social, that more or less
debarred perfect unity of thought and sympathy
between North and South, and of course tended
to segregate the national life. Miss Clayton
expressed herself well on this point, and Ralph
of course gave his own best thoughts in response. The conversation thus grew in ardor,
and even bordered on a politic kind of vehe-
mence that ignores controversy. But when Miss
Clayton declared herself most of all tried in
seeing that even the churches of the two sections could not be of one heart and one mind,

and asked why the mind of Christ should not
cause the churches of Christ to think alike,
Ralph said that he must be excused from giving
any judgment on that point, as he had never
been at all identified with church matters. The
lady would not be put off so. She discerned in
her mother's guest a *gentleman ;* one who she
was sure would speak temperately and patiently
on such a matter. For this reason she endeav-
ored to lead him on. He had, she said, doubtless thought much on the subject; for no thinking man could be a living citizen of this country
at this crisis, and not exercise himself often in a
theme so vital to our social state and progress.
If he had thought more than some others he
was bound to give out his thoughts ; and even
if others had thought more than he, his fewer
thoughts might be choicer. Ralph, however,
disclaimed all right of judgment, since he was
not himself individually a Christian. If an
impression might be held as such, and not
advanced as an opinion, he would suggest that

it might be God's way to unite the churches in love as brethren, giving the same mind and judgment in spiritual matters, but leaving them to be taught by lessons of time regarding social questions inseparable from their local positions or circumstances.

But the *moral* borders very nearly on the *spiritual*," said Miss Clayton; " and indeed, the spiritual, being once inaugurated. We have a written word of God, held to be an infallible directory as to all social questions that involve morality. It would seem that it must settle for us our opinions and decisions *as churches*, and keep out these differences that so jar upon the idea of 'a habitation of God through the Spirit.' "

" I think of two facts," said Ralph, "that may be helpful here. One is that, though the Bible, being God's Word, is infallible, it does not follow that the interpretations put upon it shall be so, even in the churches, — touching points in which salvation is not involved. This seems to me a fair supposition, a probable fact, although I am not myself established in what are called the orthodox doctrines. Then again, it seems the Divine rule, to which few exceptions are allowed, that all great processes shall be worked out slowly, both in churches and nations."

" Yes," said Miss Clayton, " the idea born with Christ's nativity and announced by angels, will no doubt sometimes be realized a clothed and living fact, — ' *Peace* on earth.' Does it not reach to the harmony of all social relations? And must there not be to this end a Divine renewal of humanity, perfecting social intelligence and moral judgment? At all events," she continued, " our Saviour's idea for His *church* is that of absolute peace and oneness, ' *that the world may believe.*' His idea must be His will, and His will must be consummated. We seem a long time waiting for the millennium. Of course He could consummate it by an act of arbitrary power. I sometimes wonder if that will be the way at last."

" Few seem to be waiting for it," said Ralph dryly.

"Do you mean few Christians?" asked the young lady.

" Well,—yes," he answered, a little hesitating, " few of the many who compose the churches."

"Oh, I do not think so," she replied. " There are earnest men at work in all lands, with much prayer for God's presence and for the progress of His Gospel. And we often hear the millennium preached of and prayed for."

" There is," said Ralph, " at least I suppose there is, a great deal of réal spiritual life hidden from view. But at best it has seemed to me that those who wait for this expectation, wait for it half-forgetfully, as a thing languidly desired and a great way off."

" A great way off it may be," said Miss Clayton. " I wish it may be near."

" I might say," said Ralph, " that the question to which all this leads is the one which most concerns me at present, — the one great

12

personal question that exists between the soul and God."

"It seems a necessity of our being that that question be settled first," she replied. And, seeing that he was waiting for her to say more, she added, "But if you are desiring this reign of peace, is it not because the soul is itself at peace?"

"I am not desiring it," said Ralph. "Christ's kingdom cannot be desired unless He is Himself desired. Any who imagine that they desire the millennium but are not ready to meet Him, must be deluded."

Ralph said this with a warmth that comported well with his strong feeling, and startled Miss Clayton. She let her dark eyes fall for one instant, and then, raising them fully to his own frank, open gaze, she said, "Whenever He does come it must be to rejoice the hearts of His friends, as He used to do at Bethany; only not in humiliation, but in glory."

At this juncture Mr. Clayton entered, and

after greeting Mrs. Stanley, was presented in turn to Mrs. Cushing and to Ralph, both of whom he received with a heartiness certainly cordial, but somewhat too brusque for elegance. He, however, wore an ease that kept every one else at ease, — the ease of a large and kindly nature. If his manner was not studied or patterned after rules, it was at least genuine, and marked by the refinement of true feeling. Knowledge of the world was one of Mr. Clayton's acquisitions which he wore on the outside. Everybody could see that he possessed it. There were many things in the world that he disliked, and nearly as many that he despised; but on the whole he liked the world very well, and the world generally liked him. The world of science was only a distant acquaintance of his; but the world of business and politics, of music, literature, and art, the world of fashion and the religious world, — all these were intimate and about equally valued friends. It must be very nearly, if not quite, time that he had not a grudge or an ill-will toward any living thing. He used to say that there are some persons, as there are some animals and insects, who are not personally agreeable, and whom no amount of philanthropy can render so. These he would on no account molest, and he would, of course, help them out of trouble when opportunity offered, or contribute to their happiness in any desired and proper way; but if this might be at arm's length, all the happier for him. This sentiment he was wont to express, as he lived, in a humorous, rather kindly vein that amused himself and perhaps injured nobody. His entrance now so far interrupted conversation as to direct it into new channels. He very properly devoted himself to the two ladies, which movement gave Mrs. Clayton the opportunity to make Ralph's acquaintance, and left Urania free for a frolic with the children. She knew their fondness for her garden and her games, and if Janie had rabbits Urania had squirrels, which Janie must by all means see. Of croquet there was none in those days, and there was no velocipede for Frank ; nevertheless both Frank and his sister were always well entertained by Urania. Indeed Frank, manly boy though he was, felt more at home in Miss Urania's society than in that of her brothers, whom he, therefore, did not particularly miss. This might have been because there was more in her nature like his own, and which understood his ; or perhaps only because she was at more pains to entertain him. The eldest of her two brothers may have been twenty-three or four ; her senior by two or three years. The other was but eighteen. Herbert, the eldest, happily had a good English name, which befell him from the fact that his father and grandfather had borne the same. But the younger brother, Orpheus, was the victim of the odd parental conceit that in his case, as in his sister's, had done what it could to flatter the myths of Greece. This trait of Mr. Clayton's may have been inherited. At all events his own only sister bore the name of Penelope, foi

which her parents must have been responsible.
The name of Orpheus, however, suited the youth
better than it could have suited his brother, —
better, even, than Urania's fitted her. Herbert
was much like his father, although taller; somewhat more deliberate; even less imaginative.
Purely practical, full of stolid energy and decision; given to study, but only to that which
he considered of use, as mathematics, architect-
ure, mechanics, and so much of chemistry as
was worth while to intelligent agriculture. Orpheus, on the other hand, was lightly built, and
of light, regular features; hated business; was
fond enough of historic and scientific studies, but
was under the ruling passion of music.

Mrs. Clayton, thinking that her guests looked
weary, would not at all allow them to return
without some refreshment, and accordingly sent
orders for an early tea, — for the evenings were
growing cooler, and Mrs. Cushing's favored
moonlight had dropped out of the evening *role*
just then. The lady then finding that they

would be delighted to walk over the grounds and herself wishing to see the children at their sports, they all sallied out. Instead of lions on the door-steps, were a stone Cerberus on one side and an eagle opposite, the coupling of which nearly overturned Ralph's gravity. His rich fun was always alive, and often troublesome. Everything in the house and over the finely-arranged premises endured some Grecian sage or deity. Apollos, Minervas, Ariadnes; busts of Homer, and Sophocles, and Plato; and so on indefinitely. Fountains swarming with Cupids intent upon hitting somebody. All this in the presence of a horticultural art certainly unknown to the ancients, and in the absence of anything else suggestive of Christian culture or modern life. " Really," thought Ralph, "a fortune were a small price to pay for a genuine taste."

But Ralph, as well as his mother, was interested in much that they saw peculiar in Southern homesteads, and differing also from anything seen at Mrs. Stanley's because of the different character of the plantation and the large number of " operations " in progress. They came upon the children in a great state of enjoyment with Urania. But most of all they observed some of the negro cabins, at a short distance rearward to the house, half-screened by clumps of box-wood and cedar, and reached by smooth pebble walks of white and gray. Ralph had to acknowledge that everything was faultlessly kept. Mrs. Clayton suggested that her Northern guests might like to walk toward the negro quarters. This they were very willing to do. Mrs. Stanley kept but few servants, and they had never seen genuine plantation-life. The children had joined them with Urania, and thus there was quite a procession. Janie could not walk without Cousin Ralph's hand, — which was only one of many proofs given him since their first walk together that nothing then said had frightened her from him. She now gave him much of her sweet prattle, and he gave her his whole attention. Mary and Frank and herself had been playing one game and another with Urania, and had seen her squirrels. " And oh, Cousin Ralph ! " she said, " the squirrels are a great deal funnier than my rabbits, and have prettier ways. They seem more like *persons.* Such warm nests they make in such warm places ! My rabbits are ever so pretty, but they are always dipping, *dipping.* Then those squirrels jump and climb so gracefully ; but how a rabbit does look when he tries to jump ! And the prettiest of all is these long, bushy tails, that are never in the way like Rex's tail. There seems to have been some mistake about my rabbits' tails ; don't you think so, Cousin Ralph ? " she asked, pausing dreamily, as the child always did when a new thought struck her.

" Why, no, little Janie," said Ralph, " not a mistake, I think. There is no doubt a perfect reason why they are just as they are."

" Oh, I know what you mean," said Janie. " There could be no mistake in what God makes, just as there could be no mistakes in what He says. All is good and all is true. And now that I think, I am sure a long, bushy tail wouldn't look very well on a rabbit," and Janie's laugh rang out like a silver bell as the idea pictured itself before her. Mrs. Cushing and the Claytons started with surprised pleasure at the merry peal, unlike any child-laughter that they knew besides. Mr. Clayton and the three ladies were walking in advance, and behind Ralph and Janie were the older children with Urania.

"That is a good thought," said Ralph, "but that is not all. The rabbit would have no *use* for the squirrel's tail. His motions are so different that it would be greatly in his way, a sad inconvenience to him. And then, as he is always down among the things that grow lowest, — finding his pleasure and his occupation on the ground, a bushy tail would get extremely dirty."

"Yes," said Janie, "his bob-tail is the neatest possible, after all."

" A thing is always prettier where it fits best," said Ralph.

.   .   .   .

They were now close upon one of the cabins, under the shade of an old oak-tree. Its sleek denizen, "Aunt Eve," was making ready the supper for her good man "Uncle Israel," who, with several of the other " hands," had come in with an overseer earlier than usual for some work on the immediate premises. Aunt Eve curtsied in the doorway as the party was passing, and received in return a sort of choral salutation, of which the predominant words, " Well, Aunt Eve, tidy as ever in your cabin," were in Mr. Clayton's voice. The tidy black creature was pleased to see that Missus Clayton had so many gentry-folks to inspect the mentioned neatness of her quarters, and declared, in a modest respectful manner and satisfied tone, that Israel junior would go with her to the house this evening to carry " the lightest pastry and the snowiest linen that ever Missus Clayton could wish to see."

As they passed on they neared others of the cabins, all neatly kept after Aunt Eve's example, and Mrs. Clayton's frequent injunction and showing. Returning to the house, they passed near where the work was in progress; four or five of the men in a group. Ralph drew attention to two striking faces among them, equally forcible yet in singular contrast. The one was that of a tall, rather awkwardly formed man; the strong face marked by regular, well-cut features, and strong expression of honest will and of earnest submission to a destiny that must be worked out on principle. The other face was of a younger man, a shade lighter and a trifle less wiry; with features more animal, yet hardly less intelligent, marked by an animus intensely evil. The first, Urania said, was Uncle Israel. The other was a man called *Joe*, a field-hand who had not been long on the place.

"We can't make him out," she said. "He is always sullen, and seems opposed to every good influence. I am half sorry papa has him; but we may be able to do him good. I dare say he has had a hard lot. And we must confess that some of those poor creatures do have a bitter history. Some think this is inevitable to the system ; and others, you know, do not."

" A prevailing impression at the North," said Ralph, " an impression that I think exists without regard to party, is that the blacks at the South are very generally Christians — that they are, as it were, constitutionally religious."

" Oh dear, no ! " said Urania, " not in any right sense. They are constitutionally emotional ; and where pains is taken with them they seem readily open to religious impressions. But there are comparatively few in whom the conscience seems really awake, and the heart with Jesus. A great many blacks, as whites also, speak his name : but we look to see it spoken out of a full heart — the life corresponding."

" After all " said Ralph, " the life is the confession."

" No, I think not," said Urania ; " I would

rather say the life is the witness to the truth or falsenesss of the confession. If an Englishman is loyal to his sovereign he *says so.* And then his life demonstrates it. And he does not say so *once*, as a matter of necessity or propriety ; never again mentioning the sovereign's name. The same loyalty that regulates his life leads to evident loyalty of speech ; and the name supremely honored will be often fittingly mentioned."

" I do not undertake to answer you," said Ralph. " Indeed my own feeling is that you are right. Still there is much to which this subject leads that is not plain to me. I am glad to listen."

" The illustration is of course incomplete," said Urania ; " good only as far as it goes. It seems to me that when Christ is received in all His blessed claims, it is because we find, — not always knowing how, — that He is personally necessary to us in just those relations which His claims qualify Him to fill. For instance : we find that we are absolutely weak and dependent.

We thus need a Sovereign Lord who cares for us and can do all things. This is Jesus. We find that we are involved in sin beyond remedy. We then need an Almighty Saviour. This is Jesus. And so on, through all the relations that He fills to His people. When He is so received we receive of His Spirit, of His mind. We thus begin to think as God thinks, and what Christ says *satisfies;* we do not need it refuted. It is doutless His good will to be confessed ; and that in the most ample sense. But it is hardly in good taste to argue the point. When He is received He *is* confessed."

Ralph was silent for a moment. And Urania, feeling that to offer apology for having said so much would seem like apologizing for the truth, was silent also. Presently Ralph said, —

" You have discovered that these subjects interest me. But, let me ask, does the individual receive Christ in all His claims because convinced that He is *just thus necessary* to us ? Is the process so logical as that ? "

" I did not intend to be understood logically, but *vitally*," said Urania; " my remark may have been badly constructed. I believe that when any soul receives the Lord, the Saviour, it is because He is *revealed* to the soul; to the heart; to the understanding. The whole man is ' drawn.' There is a renewed mind ; a birth from above, a new creature in Christ. On the part of the individual, no amount of analysis or reasoning can affect the matter. The relation of the believer to the Saviour is a *conscious* relation. No doubt it may be logical also."

" Yes, I thought so," said Ralph.

The change in his tone surprised her. It was not of irony ; neither exactly of acquiescence. It was as of one unsettled, and under some shadow of a sorrow altogether manly, and too quiet to obtrude itself.

But the party had left the pebbled walks, and were thrown more together again ; stepping over the lawn toward the house. The conversation thus became more general, and Ralph found himself by Mrs. Clayton, with Janie again pulling at his hand.

13

CHAPTER XI.

LIGHT.

THE drive home was enjoyed by all because of the pleasant way they went, and especially because all were in a mood to enjoy. They were, however, a little later than they had intended to be; so that the short Southern twilight was fast fading before they reached home. Mrs. Cushing had proposed taking Janie with them in the carriage, as she knew that Mrs. Stanley would feel better to have Ralph with Frank, since it was growing dark; beside which, Ralph was fond of the children and would doubtless be glad of the change.

(194)

Ralph's quick true feeling discerned that he could not do otherwise; and accordingly, although really preferring the first arrangement, he said cordially, and in his own droll way, at once comic and elegant,—

"By all means. Anything for a change, and for your service, Cousin Cecilia. I shall feel honored in charge of your infants; and they always treat me well."

Mrs. Stanley accepted the proposal, and as they drove away (Frank, of course, driving the pony) Ralph said,—

"Don't mind what I said, Franky, we are all infants in our mother's eyes, you know."

"I don't mind," said Frank, "only you can't have these reins. This is my establishment. Let me alone, and I don't mind what you say. But May here is a real stuck up old woman. She will be pointing at you, cousin Ralph,"

"Oh Franky, Franky! your manners are not improving," said Mary.

"There, cousin Ralph, don't you see? It is

something about *manners* from morning to night. When it isn't manners it is *morals*. Oh, May, when did you grow up?"

"Don't you think he is a tease, Cousin Ralph?" "But after all, he is a first-rate fellow," she said, patting him with real fondness. "The best brother, for a little one, in all Tennessee, I believe."

"Now May, sister May!" said the really sensitive Frank. "I *will* stop teasing you if you will only stop your compliments. Nevertheless, May, your manner-and-moral lectures are a severe trial to me; a real thorn in the flesh," said he, with mock pathos.

"Oh brother, you *mischief!* you do stop teasing, indeed. Suppose now we give Cousin Ralph a chance to speak."

"Oh! for manners! Yes for manners' sake we will," said the boy. "Now cousin Ralph, here is your chance. Please adapt your speech to Mary's grown-up comprehension."

They were driving on at a good rate; keeping

close to the carriage, which Zed caused to roll rapidly. Ralph was too well entertained to care. about being heard himself. "You are doing very well," he said, " both in your talking and driving. The pony has something to do o keep up with the carriage to-night. They are getting you home in time for your history lesson, Franky."

" Pray don't suggest history!" gasped Frank. " It will be endured when it comes."

" There is a star!" exclaimed Mary. " Just above the sunset glow. How bright! how lovely!"

"Yes," said Ralph, "it is indeed. We always look for the evening star at home. I dare say father and Rebekah are looking at it now."

" Now *there* is a grand study for us," said Frank. " That star served me a good turn, to help me forget my history lesson. Astronomy must be grand!"

" Yes, you are right enough there," said Ralph. " But certain astronomical *facts* are all that you could gain until you have acquired a good deal of mathematics. Just so the science of history is grander, but requires greater study, than the memorizing of bare *facts* in history. What do you know of either?"

"Not much," said Frank, coloring. "I am going into algebra next year, but I don't know when I can take geometry. History takes so much time, when a fellow might be learning some of these good things!"

"But," said Ralph, "you *could* not, and would not *wish* to grow up ignorant of history. There is time for all."

"Oh, I suppose so!" said Frank dolefully. "But it takes so long to grow up! Except Mary,— hush now, May! Cousin Ralph, is the evening star a star or a planet?"

"A planet, in some sense a star," said Ralph, "though the stars are not planets. The evening star, so called, is properly the planet Venus."

There was a brief silence, and Mary asked

thoughtfully, "What is light? It must be *something*."

"Mary, *you* are a philosopher!" cried Frank. "Oh, Mary! something must be something! The something that we see by, and almost exist by; the something that reveals the world, — that, they say, gives color, and form, and all beauty; this something that we call light, — why, it must *be something!* How profound!"

"Franky, now you promised not to tease me."

"I am not teasing, Mary. I say I am going to propose your name as a member of the National Scientific Society."

"Come Franky! you never can stop. Cousin Ralph, will you please to tell us what light is?"

Ralph explained to them in as simple words and as few as possible, the "undulating theory," namely, that *light* is *motion;* a peculiar mode of motion, consisting in an inconceivably rapid series of undulations, or waves, of an invisible fluid without appreciable weight or substance, that fills all space. "These undulations," he

said, " are perceived by the eye, as the undulations of the air are perceived by the ear. Tho
one is light; the other is sound. Light, then,
objectively, is *motion*. Subjectively, as regards
the observer, it is *sensation*. The invisible fluid
which is the medium of this is called *ether*."

" What sets all this going, Cousin Ralph ? "
asked Frank. " What starts the waves?   And
how is it that they are everywhere when it is
light, and nowhere when it is dark?"

Ralph laughed. " Your last question," he
said, " arises from a wrong impression that it
would take time to correct.   As to the first, you
must remember that undulation is motion of
form, not of matter.   Thus, if you place a straw
or a cork on the surface of smooth water, and
then disturb the water by throwing a pebble
near the floating substance, you will see that this
does not move outward with the undulations,
showing that the water itself does not progress
outward, only that there is a progressive change
of form.   In like manner, those active processes

that are at work between the particles of luminous bodies, agitate the ether, as your pebble
agitates the water; and the agitation is expressed in undulations, of which the undulations
of water are a correct but an exceedingly coarso
illustration."

" But the rays of light seem to come in
straight lines," said Mary, "and the water
moves in circles."

" The undulations move in right lines as regards any object that they shine (or fall) upon,"
said Ralph. " But if we could stand at the
point from which they proceed, we would see
that they move equally in all directions; that is,
in circles as regards the centre."

" Is all this *proved?* " asked the practical
Frank. " My teacher says that a theory is good
for nothing unless induced from facts."

" This theory of light originated," said Ralph,
" before the most wonderful facts now known
about light were established. It originated as
being one of the only two theories conceiv

able for examining light on any physical basis. But the longer the phenomena of light
are studied, the stronger is the support given to
this theory. Philosophers are so delighted with
its uniform explanation of facts, that there is
no longer any disposition to dispute its correct-
ness."

"People pretend to know how fast light
travels," said Mary. "Ever so many miles in
one second."

"That," said Ralph, "is the discovery of a
Danish astronomer named *Rœmer*. He noticed
that an eclipse of one of the moons of Jupiter,
observed when the earth is at that point of its
own orbit nearest to Jupiter, returned sixteen
minutes *later than calculated* when the earth was
at the opposite part of the orbit, — that is, about
two hundred million miles farther from Jupiter
than before. These calculations for the real return of the eclipse were found correct beyond
all controversy. Its *observed* return was, therefore, sixteen minutes too late. It follows then,

that an eclipse of one of these satellites that would be seen by us at a certain time when we are nearest Jupiter, is seen sixteen minutes (or about one thousand seconds) later when we are two hundred million miles farther away. This gives to light a velocity of two hundred thousand miles in one second."

"Then," exclaimed Frank, delighted, "we can tell how long it takes light to come to us from the stars."

"Yes," answered Ralph, "provided we can calculate the distances of the stars. In the case of one or more of them this has been done by actual measurement. And, upon the basis of this known distance of the nearest, Herschel worked out his method of computing distances by magnitudes."

"How far from us are they?" asked Frank. "And *what* are they, anyhow?"

Ralph laughed again. "Your questions come too fast," he said. "As to the distances, some of them are so great that they only bewilder us.

We really seem no better informed after knowing all about it. The first whose distance was
actually measured (doubtless one of the very
nearest), is six hundred thousand times farther
from us than our own sun ; and a wave of light
starting from it at this moment, will reach us in
about ten years. But some of them are hundreds of times farther from us than this."

"Ten years!" exclaimed Mary. "And hundreds of ten years! To think that the undulations should keep on so long. How very singular."

"Yes truly," said Ralph. "And the rapidity
of this light-motion, as compared with all ordinary physical motion known to us, is proved to
be inconceivable by comparing it with other ve-
locities. For instance: a cannon-ball is com-
puted 'to move at the rate of about five
hundred miles an hour. Now, aim your cannon
at the star we speak of, and suppose the ball,
never to fall back to the earth, but to keep
right on at five hundred miles an hour. It will,

at that rate, reach the star only after about *fourteen million years.* But the light waves pass from the star to us in *ten* years. So then, those little waves of ether of which the eye is sensible, move many thousand times faster than a cannon-ball."

"How wonderful!" said Frank. "Mary, I'll have to thank you after all for your inquiry, and commend your conclusion. Light *is* something, sure enough. We hear of ethereal beauty, ethereal lightness, and so on. I think we must begin to talk of ethereal swiftness, and ethereal distances. But, Cousin Ralph, how do we really know and prove all these facts?"

"By different means," said Ralph. "Greatly by means of Geometry. Of course in some sense *the telescope* has done everything for astromony. Yet it was in some good sense a science before we had the telescope. The law of gravitation being understood, and the telescope in hand, this might have sufficed to reduce star-gazing to a system, but after all, the calculations which *consolidate* the system, and give it compactness as a science, are due to Geometry."

"Then," said Frank, "I must get into geometry as soon as ever I can."

"Better systematize your history, first," said Ralph.

And as they turned into the Stanley grounds, and the pony walked slowly up the carriage-way, Mary said, —

"Mamma thinks that the works of God not only prove Him holy, and loving, and good, but prove Him in every sense *absolute.* We can't find that He has made a mistake, or fallen short of any design, or ever grown weary. That seems to me a nice thought."

"Yes," said Frank, "mother has ever so many nice thoughts. What was that the other day, May, about 'God infinite?'"

"Oh! I *tried* to remember," said Mary. "It was something like this: That the God who redeemed is the God who created, for only the

Creator could redeem a fallen creation. That Redemption, then, is as infinite as Creation. That God being in all things absolute, as He is infinite, it follows that everything which He says is not only infinitely said but absolutely sure. God having spoken in grace, can neither retract nor fail."

" And," said Frank, " she said that this is the stability of the Christian. God, having promised, will surely fulfil. His written word, she said, proves itself of Him as clearly as His works do."

" All these sentiments are what good Parson Laidley at home would call ' excellent points,' " said Ralph. " And," he continued, as they drove up to the door, " I must consider your part of the discourse better than mine."

.   .   .   .

Franky went to his history and his Latin. Janie had a deal to tell Ralph about the drive after those two fine horses, — " and with a white man to drive. It seemed so fine and so strange!" And Mary had a story for her mother of the wonders they had been discussing with Ralph.

"Cousin Ralph was very good to tell you so much, and at so much pains," said her mother.

. . . .

The daily reading at Mrs. Stanley's was in the evening; being so preferred by her. She used to say that our Father's thoughts toward us being for our refreshment, should be read when we are weary, and, being for our instruction, should be read when we are most at leisure from other things. That was her own feeling; but others might find some earlier part of the day giving larger, happier room to the sayings that are faithful and true. This evening the words from Deuteronomy, "Oh, that there were such an heart in them, that they would fear me, and keep all my commandments always," considered in connection with the words of Jesus: "If ye love me keep my commandments," were realized by Ralph as expressive not only of good will, but also of *love* as we understand it, on God's part towara His people; and of His desire for the love of the ones loved. And in the conversation that followed, (the children having retired) Ralph gave some outline of his conversation with Urania Clayton.

" How God *waits* to be gracious to them that resist Him ! " said Mrs. Stanley. " We need to remember that the wrath of God is not vindictive. He delights in mercy ; *not* in the death of the sinner. Judgment is His 'strange works,' but it is part of His perfect doing."

The remark was not pointed at Ralph, but he perhaps thought it was. He answered rather abruptly, " I never found an explanation of eternal judgment as coinciding with eternal love."

" Not in the cross ? " asked Mrs. Stanley.

Ralph did not answer; and his mother said, " Faith rests in God, and does not seek for explanations that He is not pleased to give. Our Saviour certainly is not playing with us, nor with words, when He uses not figures only, but

14

declarations on this point. But there is no delight in them. God is love. God is the Judge. God the Redeemer is God the Sovereign, the Holy. When His judgments are in the earth they will be *right* judgments."

"Yes," said Ralph, "I suppose that must be so. And the answer of an evil conscience is after all the best answer to the problem. The one question pressing me, you know, is, how shall a man be justified? The very rising of the question seems to justify God."

Mrs. Stanley looked up from her needle-work. "I did not know that you were not satisfied as to that, Cousin Ralph," she said.

"Oh, I know the orthodox doctrine," said Ralph; "and I do not altogether repudiate it. But I am not clear about the blood-shedding; and I am sensible that Christ is not all to me that He is fitted to be, nor His peace my possession."

"That last is not strange, if the shedding of His blood has no meaning to you," said Mrs

Stanley. "Then where do you find atone-ment?"

"I am assured," said Ralph, "that He in some way gave himself for us that He might redeem us from all iniquity. And if I were assured as to the Divine necessity of a perfect demonstration of the Divine justice on account of sin, then I dare say I should see how perfectly the sorrow and darkness and death of the Son of God in flesh will meet the case."

"If Jesus be indeed the Son of God," said Mrs. Stanley, "there could be no other meaning in His death than Atonement; it is impossible. But, Cousin Ralph, let me say that you are simply yielding to a temptation, or to some pride of intellect, in all this. If you are convinced that the crucified Jesus is risen again, declared to be the Son of God with power, it is because God has convinced you of it — has *taught* you. Yet I do not see that you *are* convinced. That is — your heart is not holding this truth, and worshipping Him. If it were there would be neither cavilling nor stumbling at the meaning of His sacrifice."

" I do recognize His claims as Divine," said Ralph.

" My dear cousin," said Mrs. Stanley, " you may think that you recognize in Jesus the Son of God. But recognizing is not believing. When you get the view of Him and of His work that God gives, your heart will be broken ; it may be with pain, it may be with rapture ; but, in either case, you will know that it is broken, and that the blind eyes see."

.   .   .   .   .   .

As Ralph was retiring that night he turned to some words from Thomas a Kempis that had held his eye in the quiet moment after dinner, and had lain in his thought all day : ' Blessed and true is that comfort that is inwardly received from *the truth.* A devout man always carries about with him Jesus his comforter, and saith to Him, ' Be with me, O Lord Jesus, in all places and at all times.'

"I have never experienced that," thought Ralph; "I do not know that. No, *I do not.*"

CHAPTER XII.

VISIT TO THE ORPHANS.

IT was on this same evening that a scene transpired in the 'pretty white house,' as Ralph always called the Jamesons' domicile; some record of which must here be given.

Mrs. Jameson, the mother of 'the young preacher,' was sitting with her daughter Alice, who was somewhat older than Frederick. Mother and daughter were busy with their needle-work. The apartment was an extreme one in several respects. It was at the extreme of the north wing; and was of extreme neat

(214)

ness, and extremely plain in its furnishing. Although there were many other rooms in the house, some of which were large, and one at least having better adornments, this one was found most convenient for general use. The neat kitchen with its waxed floor opened off on the left; and, there being no servant claiming rule, the proximity was altogether to be preferred. This apartment served as dining-room, (or rather as breakfast, dinner and supper-room,) sewing-room for the two just introduced, and study for Frederick and the growing Robert. It was the very life of these four to live within sight and sound of one another's look and voice. The busy Frederick was all day at his fruit-nursery and orchard, or at some business connected therewith; or at his profitable recreation of cabinet work. And Robert was helping him when not at school. Thus the evening was Fred's only time either for the society of mother and sister, or for the studies which also made so large part of his existence. As he was possessed of one of those rare, happy temperaments that allows its owner to read or think without complete isolation from others of mortal kind, it fell out that the family room and the study stood one and undivided.

Mrs. Jameson was elderly, not old ; above the medium height, but well proportioned, with a face that must have been once beautiful, now only slightly lined with care. Her well-arranged hair was fine and soft, with all the enviable beauty of a luxuriant gray. Her deeply-set eyes were a soft hazel, and her hands slender, delicate, and of a texture and touch that could belong only to a lady. Her whole appearance rendered it quite superfluous that any one seeing her be told of her genuine culture and self-respect. And, before knowing her long, one would discover that these qualities, (in-born and in-wrought as they were), were co-existent with genial sweetness, with humility, and with a truly catholic delight in realizing brotherhood with all mankind. This was the woman who had borne and reared Frederick Jameson, and by means of whose teaching and example he had imbibed his first love of the truth as it is in Jesus. The daughter was not much like the mother. Although she was fond of her mother and of Frederick, yet her natural fondness had not at all times by any means either concealed or controlled her enmity to the Christian living of the others. It was only lately that she had withdrawn from an attitude and an occasional outspoken impatience that amounted to a phase of persecution; and, finding that she was not only unlovely but really herself miserable, had softened, and at length allowed some faithful word from her mother, kindly urged, to open her eyes and her heart before the very cross of Christ. From that time her strong, natural affection found no hindrance. Frederick, whom she had really ardently loved, became her great help, and, next to the mother, her chief source of solicitude and of joy. But Robert, seventeen years old, who had always been the baby and the pet, was loved with a peculiar love. Since the enmity had been destroyed, and that hardness and hatred toward the truth, which divides so many households, had been taken away, no more peaceful and united family could be found.

. . . .

"Alice, dear, what can keep Fred and Robie so long out?" asked Mrs. Jameson. "They went only those few rods, the short way through the brush-wood, to Mr. Smith's, with the book-shelves, meaning to return at once, I think."

"Sure enough, it is too long," said Alice. "Oh, I dare say they found some one there whom they know. Mr. Smith, if alone, would hardly invite them to stay."

"Mr. Smith is a hard man, truly," said the mother. "But, you know, he has had a hard life. Alone so many years, and not sustained by anything unseen! How could there be any expansiveness without any sunshine?"

"Oh, mother, he was just so years and years ago, before his wife and baby died."

"*Somewhat* so," said Mrs. Jameson. "Yes, he is naturally morose."

. . . .

At this moment the two young men entered, accompanied by Orpheus Clayton, who, by reason of a common love for music, (and by other tastes in common) had been strongly bound to Robert from childhood. Robert was in high glee at having found Orpheus at Mr. Smith's, entertaining "the old man," with a new composition for the flute. "One of his own, mother. There is no music that smoothes out Smith's crabbedness like Orpheus Clayton's."

Orpheus blushed slightly at this; for Robert had spoken more proudly than if it had been some success of his own.

"I am glad to see you Orpheus," said Mrs. Jameson. "The more so that we had not expected you. A pleasure is always enriched by surprise."

"You are very kind, Mrs. Jameson," said the

young man. "If my coming gives you pleasure
I must preserve its quality by not coming too
often."

"Ah! you always have a ready answer," said
Mrs. Jameson with a quiet laugh that told of
deep enjoyment. "Are your father and mother
well? and your sister?"

"Very well; yes ma'am, thank you. I came
this way with Herbert this afternoon. He had
some business for father at Mr. Wayland's, and
afterward we rode around by Mr. Smith's to
conclude arrangements for letting out Joe.
Mrs. Smith, who is always in love with my flute,
and fancies to have me blow on his when mine
is not at hand, would have me stay and *sup* with
him, as he calls drinking tea."

"You must have done him good," said Frederick. "He has never, I believe, smiled so
entirely, or been so talkative, as this evening."

"The old man has a warm spot around his
heart somewhere," said Robert. "The spark
only needs to be fanned the right way."

"Why do you call him 'the old man,' Robie?" said Mrs. Jameson. "He is not old, and the expression, as you use it, is rude."

"Oh, it is convenient, mother, and it describes him very well, I think. But, if you don't like to hear it, I'll not say it."

Mrs. Jameson knew that the two youths were 'up to music,' as Frederick was wont to call the working of their ruling passion, and she gave them the opportunity to hold their own converse while she asked Frederick further about their call at Mr. Smith's.

"It does seem to me," he said, "that God is drawing that hard, strange man to Himself by ways of singular tenderness. It has led me to think that traits which seem to us to mark certain individuals as peculiarly evil, may be only the working of constitutional habit from which others are constitutionally free. If God judges so, and is dealing with this hardness as an infirmity demanding compassion as well as correction, He is so reproving the uncharity of our impatience."

"You are giving me quite a lecture, brother," said Alice. "You know I am not at all patient with Mr. Smith. He snaps so! One can better bear with the great bark of a great dog."

"There is something large about his nature, notwithstanding," replied Frederick. "I have seen it in many ways. But just to think how this short acquaintance with Orpheus has been used for his good, and for the bringing out of his large qualities! It is not the *music* only, for he will *talk with him* by the hour."

There was a moment's pause, and then, as Fred Jameson always told his mother everything, he continued: "Mr. Smith asked me this evening where I am going to speak next Sunday, and said he should like to be there. It is the first time he has said any kind word about it."

This was true, but it was not all the truth. Mr. Smith had often made *un*kind remarks on the subject of his young neighbor's course,— remarks that had been no small trial to Frederick. The exclamations of good sympathy from mother and sister at what he now said, were natural. Perhaps, also, they were gracious. Frederick responded, —

"I am glad also, — glad that the enmity is breaking down; especially (indeed I may say only) because, in as far as I am speaking the true words of God, it indicates the breaking of the enmity toward Him."

"Do you not speak anywhere before Sunday?"

"Not this week. Next week, if God please, in the new church at Kenyonville."

Orpheus caught the last words, and said, "Frederick, Mr. Smith says that a man who preaches the Gospel ought to do nothing else."

"That is a strange remark for Mr. Smith," said Mrs. Jameson. "He has always had a good deal to say in disapproval of the clerical profession, as he calls the ministry."

"Mr. Smith is both right and wrong, I dare say," said Frederick thoughtfully, adding, "I think cases do arise in the ordering of God where one is called to some work as an Evangelist without wisdom for a pastoral charge. 'Some, evangelists; some, pastors and teachers.'"

"*I* would like to see you *all minister*," said Orpheus.

"Oh, *I* wouldn't!" said Robert. "He wouldn't seem like Fred. Think of him in a white neck-cloth, and a long-tailed black frock! Oh, Fred! And then, what should I do if you were in a parsonage and I alone here?"

The ardent Robert had taken alarm in such funny earnest, that all present laughed with a gusto which partly re-assured him.

"Rob, the case is plain enough," said Frederick. "The Lord, no doubt, has foreseen and noted all our past, and his good hand has been in it. He makes our gifts and capacities just what they are, and our circumstances are of His ordering or allowance. Here are mother and sister to be supported; and if I am sure of anything as to the present, it is that these hands must work."

"How can a man always know what God's call is?" asked Orpheus, addressing Mrs. Jameson.

"I hardly know how to answer you," she said. "I think sometimes, perhaps generally, the will of God as to our course is so evident that one cannot but know it, if the heart is attentive to learn God's will and not intent upon its own. In case of any unusual conflict or perplexity, the believing soul will not be in haste."

The youth paused before replying: "And then they say '*Pray.*' Frederick believes in prayer, and so does Rob. And I think I do, also."

"Without any argument on that point," said Mrs. Jameson, "it is sufficient now to say that the child of God who has his Saviour's fellowship cannot live without prayer, nor forego it; either on his own account, or on account of his brethren, or of the kingdom of God. God's thoughts about it are no doubt higher and

15

sweeter than the reasoning of men. In one view it is presented as a test of obedience. Pray because God says so. That might be enough of itself. But it is presented also on a higher plane; 'Praying *in the Holy Spirit.*' 'Praying always with all prayer and supplication *in the Spirit.*' This is not mere obedience. It is communion with God. And it may well lead us to watch lest we *make* prayers, instead of being so filled with the Spirit that they are wrought in us."

"Albeit," said Frederick, "the highest, sweetest, only service toward God *is* obedience; unquestioning, filial doing of what is bidden."

"Yes; the word *filial* embracing love and understanding," said his mother. "For 'the end of the commandment is *love*, out of a pure heart, of a good conscience, and of faith unfeigned.' And the growth of a child of God is in wisdom and understanding."

.   .   .   .

A day or two after this, Herbert and Orpheus

Clayton drove over to the Stanleys to pay their compliments to Ralph whose visit they had missed; bringing messages to the ladies from their mother, who was that day unable to accompany them. Ralph thought he had never seen a contrast more emphatic between two brothers; but found them both well-informed, agreeable young gentlemen, whom he was glad to know. Mrs. Stanley came in to see them; and while Herbert was conversing with her, Ralph went over with Orpheus the adventure that followed the breaking down of the carriage, which led Orpheus to speak of his own acquaintance with the Jamesons and of his recent evening with them. Frederick had been several times spoken of by Mrs. Stanley with a desire that her friends might know him, and Ralph was glad to know of the appointment at Kenyonville. The Clayton brothers withdrew soon, declining an invitation to dinner, and feeling that they had made an acquaintance, whom they could not fail to value. For those two brothers, though so unlike, were yet unlike in a way that assimilates, and drew strongly together in many of their tastes.

It fell out, by-the-by, that Ralph met with Frederick Jameson before hearing him at Kenyonville. At dinner that day he spoke of young Clayton's acquaintance with the family, and of his apparently ardent friendship for Robert, of whom Ralph had not heard. Mrs Stanley proposed that they should, on the day following, drive on the Nashville road, and call at Mrs. Jameson's. Mr. Stanley and Mr. Jameson had been close friends, and the two ladies esteemed each other cordially, but seldom met; as Mrs. Jameson was unable to pay visits. Mrs. Stanley would feel quite free to take her friends there.

This was agreed to by all except Mary, who, if her mamma would allow her, would prefer staying at home. She did not like Alice Jameson; was sure she *never could* like her; and really felt every way uncomfortable at the

Jamesons'. Frank was disposed to take this as a personal affront, as *he* considered the Jamesons (all except Alice) the most delightful acquaintances. And what if Alice was plain, and inexpressive, and lacking all tact in entertaining? She was a good soul who injured nobody; and there must be something to her, since she was always careful of her mother, and her brothers were very fond of her. Mary thought this very probable, but did not see how those commendable qualities, in a person whom she did not like, could at all affect the case in point. She did not like Alice Jameson, and Alice Jameson certainly was not agreeable to strangers.

Mrs. Stanley gently checked the children; saying that they were speaking too much, and that personal criticism with no good end in view is quite out of taste. They begged their mamma's pardon, and the conversation was led by her in a way of more general interest. But after dinner, the three children being together in one corner of the library, Frank, with some polite reserve, opened his batteries on poor May.

"I think you are quite too bad, May," he said, "Mamma says we should have charity for all."

"Yes. I *have* charity for Alice," said Mary, not out of patience, but quite in earnest. "I wouldn't harm her, and I would be willing to do her good. But what is the harm of not going to see her? I *don't* like her, and I *can't help it.* She is a good creature, I dare say; but if she is, let her prove it by making herself agreeable, like Urania Clayton or Ursula Farr."

"Comparisons are not good, May darling," said their mother, as she was cutting some flowers near them. "Be gentle, my dear daughter, in your feelings, and in the expression of them."

"Yes, mamma," replied Mary. "But just think, mamma, how impossible it is to like what one dislikes."

"Oh, May, May! grown-up May!" said

Frank. "Philosophy again, and *such* philosophy!"

"Gentle, Franky,—no teasing," said Mrs Stanley, adding to Mary, "You may not like qualities that are opposed to your tastes. But respect and love are quite disconnected from what is essentially agreeable. I can tell you my dear, that Alice is more deserving of your regards than Cousin Ursula."

"Why, mamma! how is that possible? I think Ursula is lovely."

"Ursula has an agreeable manner with those whom she seldom meets," said Mrs. Stanley, "because politeness is, with her, less a *principle* arising out of genuine good feeling and unselfish regard for others, than a *custom* in the observance of which she is conscious of appearing well. Ursula is more lovely out of her home than in it. You do not know that she regards her own comfort first in everything; and yet continues always to make herself uncomfortable and her mother unhappy."

Mary was quite blank at this. "Oh, mamma! Why did you tell me?" she exclaimed.

"I will tell you now why I have told you this," said her mother. "You would certainly observe it yourself as you grow older; and I have anticipated your own discovery of it because it conveys just the lesson that you need at this time. You are naturally prone to form judgments on first appearances; that is, you pre-judge, and then you allow your prejudice to rule you, — caring neither to inform yourself further, nor to judge yourself wi h your neighbor. This you must take pains to correct, my dear child. For the Saviour's name you must correct it."

The tears had come in Mary's eyes, and in Frank's, too, the generous fellow instinctively feeling the reproof his sister bore. Little Janie, who was absorbed in a frolic with Rex, had heard nothing connectedly, but looked up just here, saying, "Uncle John says we ought to like everybody."

"That is not what you say, is it mamma?" said Mary beseechingly.

"No, my dear child," said her mother. "I say that qualities are inseparable from persons, and that you cannot *like* what your tastes are wholly adverse to. But you can lead that wholly unselfish life which is love, and which not only renders to all their due, but finds an interest in the happiness of all."

"Thank you, mamma, thank you really, mamma," she said, rather tremulously, but not allowing the tears to rise again. Janie noticed that there was some strong emotion transpiring ; but, apprehending that it was not her affair, drew a little sigh and went to her lessons. As Mary passed the parlor-door half an hour later, Ralph rallied her on her disposition to stay alone at home when the going out was not of her preference. "Cousin Mary," he said, "you must surely not be one of those sickly mortals who make happiness to consist in enjoying one's *self*. They ask us 'How did you *enjoy your self?*' on such an occasion; not 'what did you enjoy in others?' or 'Did you see or hear what enlarged your soul toward God and men?' This enjoying one's self can be turned into miserable work."

" Oh, Cousin Ralph!" said Mary, half-crying again; "will you make me ashamed, too? Mamma has been giving me one of her sweet scathings. And now *you!* But I *do* want to enjoy others than myself. That is just the difficulty, I don't always find *how.*"

" No, Mary, no," said Ralph quickly. "I spoke like a fool. Forgive me! I spoke like a fool."

" You had better go with us, May dear," said Mrs. Cushing. "You will have the opportunity to see the spot of our adventure, — with a new graphic description by Ralph."

" I shall go, Aunt Helen, you may be sure I shall go," she replied. "I see that I have been very wrong. Cousin Ralph, I don't think you spoke like a fool."

But their drive that afternoon was in quite another direction; to visit first an orphan school and asylum, endowed by bequest, and, in part, maintained by private charity. Mrs. Stanley wished also to visit two poor families whom she knew to be worthy and in need. All these objects of visitation by a happy coincidence lay on the Kenyonville road; by which means Zed was made sufficiently acquainted with the route for Tuesday evening.

How pleasant that visit to the orphan house was! How much one learns from beholding God's manifest faithful care of these little ones (whom His wisdom has bereaved), in the happy fruit of a little love and toil that some of our fellows, as His instruments, have been led to bestow on them. Mrs. Cushing, whose nerves had been weaker for a few days, and who had even required some nursing, was quite refreshed by what she saw, — "really fortified and comforted," she said. (She had already missed very much the opportunities of going out of her self that her home neighborhood supplied; for, although full of loving interest in her cousin's family, there was no field for benevolent action there, since the servants were, of course, not accessible to a stranger. Except, indeed, during the two hours of Sunday instruction, which was a time-honored custom on the part of the Stanleys toward their servants.)

The visit of to-day filled Mrs. Cushing's whole soul with new health. They had but a few minutes in the school-room, as the daily session was just closing. The closing exercise was one of recitations from Scripture, which also, they were informed, inaugurated the exercises of the morning. One of the texts in chorus was from the Psalm: "Seven times a day do I praise Thee, because of Thy righteous judgments."

At this point a little hand went up, and its owner being permitted to speak, a bright-eyed little fellow said, "We only give thanks to our Father morning and evening, and here it says seven times a day."

"Yes, Johnny," said the teacher. "But our action as a school is not the limit of the free service of every one of us toward our Heavenly Father. These expressions in the Psalms are the expressions of a soul happy in the forgiveness of sins and singing praises to God at all times."

" The Saviour hadn't come then, had He?" said Johnny.

" No. But there were promises and teachings indicating that a Deliverer *should* come. The Gospel was not fully revealed as now, but God's true people understood that God Himself was Saviour; and that forgiveness was of His grace, not of our merit. The Old Testament is full of this."

Another hand went up, and an older scholar asked, " How can we give thanks to God because of His judgments ? "

" Ah, Willie Jones ! " said the teacher, " Mr. Root or Mr. Jameson might give us a gracious sermon from that text. I can only say it is because the judgment of condemnation that was due to us has been taken by Jesus, in whom our sins were put away. And He Himself, the Lord, is the risen living witness of this. God's judgments are *for* us, not *against* us, if we are honoring Jesus, — if our hearts are receiving Him. The heart that loves Him knows how to praise Him for *all* His judgments, *in all things*, for they are right and good." *

A few more verses were recited, among which the one most dwelt upon was 1st John, iv. 11: " Beloved, if God so loved us, we ought also to love one another." It was shown to be a thought suited to affect only the believer in Jesus; because only *as God is believed* can His love move us to love one another. As the teacher was about dismissing them, another hand was seen signaling to speak.

" Well, Annie ? " said the teacher, patiently, " Our time is up, but we will hear you."

" May we sing 'I lay my sins on Jesus' ? " asked the child.

* Psalms cxix. 128.

The singing was generally reserved until after supper. But as eight or ten little hands went up quickly in favor of the hymn, it was thought best not to deny it. Familiar as it was to all present, it was yet so full of "the old, old story," which is always new, that every heart which had ever felt its sweetness and its power, united as in a new song of gladness and of peace.

And while the children went to their out-door recreation, the visitors were conducted over the building by a sweet-faced matron, who took a quiet delight in exhibiting the neatness and system of the establishment. "Oh, for a hand in such a work!" thought Mrs. Cushing as their conductress went over its details. Mrs. Stanley related the scene they had witnessed in the school-room, and thought the little girl's request a simple and touching one.

"Yes," said the matron, I do not think it was asked in order that strangers might hear them sing. There are so many visitors every week that the children cease to regard it as extraordinary, — almost cease to notice it. And Annie Benson is an unaffected, truthful child."

Their visit was limited, of course, but Mrs. Cushing and Ralph both felt that, in value, those forty minutes exceeded many ordinary hours. The drive was renewed with greater pleasure for the good received in seeing so many children happy. That the kind care and wise training bestowed in that orphan house was not the fruit of a dead philanthropy, but of a living faith, was too manifest to be overlooked by any who had eyes to see.

Where the Spirit of Christ is there is *the fruit of the Spirit*, and the Father is glorified for Jesus' sake.

Mrs. Cushing would not intrude upon her cousin's private charities, nor disturb the families visited, by pushing her own way among them. She would drive on with Ralph, she said; and would return that way at such time as Mrs. Stanley might be ready to join them. Less than an hour would suffice, Mrs. Stanley thought; as the two houses stood not far apart. A by-road, which she pointed out, would give them a pleasant drive of half an hour and return; in the course of which they would get a pretty view of Kenyonville a little northward. They parted, therefore, at the house of Widow Brown, whose son Ephraim was crippled these twelve years gone; and whose daughter Ellen was sole nurse and provider for Ephraim and their somewhat infirm mother. The other house was the scene and centre of a different history. It contained only two aged persons, Rufus Gray and his wife Sally. Their only son, Charles, had been but twice heard from since he " 'listed " in the army during the Mexican war, seven years before.

This Charlie Gray was then a short, cheery, popular fellow of eighteen; a full-sized man at that; the hope of his father and the joyful pride of his mother. Always a good son to them, and ambitious to be their support, he was yet restive

16

under the restraints of the tame, rustic life to
which he was born; and, in an hour of reckless
ardor, he took the fatal step that he could not
retrace. Bitter weeping followed. There was
no reproach; only deep, ungovernable grief that,
for the time, swallowed up the whole nature of
parents and son. The three wept on each other's
necks. There was a night of anguish. Then
the father said, " You must go, my son; the
Lord keep and save you and us." And the
mother kissed him, and again kissed him; and
said, " The Lord bless you, my son, and give you
back to us if it be good in His sight." And
they both forgave him freely, fully, at once and
forever, as God forgives His children. And for
their sakes Charlie cheered up for the little time
that remained; but the poor boy went out in
the bitterness of his soul. He never forgave
himself.

In him his parents had lost a noble, filial boy
and Nelly Brown a pure-minded ardent lover
He had written his parents once, just on em-

barking at New Orleans; a letter brimful of affection, and of the penitence that he could not repress, though happy in their forgiveness; and enlivened here and there by an ill-concealed enthusiasm for the adventures in prospect. (For Rufus and Sally were not so destitute then as now. The infimities of age had crept upon them rapidly since their great sorrow.) The other letter was to Nelly Brown; written on Mexican soil; with her in his heart, and a battle in prospect. His natural courage was great; he feared no evil. But no one except Nelly had supposed that Charlie Gray was a Christian Yet there was one expression in his letter to his parents that comforted them concerning this. "I believe," he said, "if the blessing of God, that you invoked for me, is given, it will come through Jesus only; for I find that I am without goodness and without strength, — though not before men." And to Nelly he had written, "A battle! Only think of going into battle — and in such a war as this! If it were in self-defence, or in defence of a good cause, it *might be* better; though bloodshed is sad and dubious work, at best. But think of giving one's life in a cause that cannot be justified! I do not doubt you are praying for me. And I am willing to tell *you* that I pray sometimes; if for myself, then be sure for you likewise, — for no distance can separate us. If *one's* self is mentioned before God, the other must be also. This for you only. Farewell."

Nelly kept the secret tenderly; conveying to his father and mother the message sent them. But when months had passed, and no word came, and hope had faded into resignation, then she felt herself released; not from her willing vows to him, but from keeping any longer that which would comfort alike all the mourners. She showed his parents all the letter; and they thanked God, and their bowed heads were lifted up.

.   .   .   .

When Mrs. Stanley alighted at the Brown

house the pony-carriage drew up also; for the children must see Nelly and Ephraim. Thus it was that Ralph and his mother pursued their drive alone. Ralph, who was always talkative, and especially so when he had his mother quite to himself, became unusually silent, and continued so until she asked him of what he was thinking.

"I was thinking," he said, "how different my reminiscences of my own boyhood would be if you were not in them; and father, and Rebekah, and all that made the old house *home.* How doleful, comparatively, how unnatural, to be able to recall no family life! to have been only a little living bit of a great institution itself alive, it may be, with all pleasant charities and useful instruction, but containing no father, no mother, everybody, everything; mine generally and loosely; nothing mine particularly, — I had almost said, nothing divinely. I can see only two divine institutions on the earth; one is the family, the other is the church. All other institutions that work good seem to me (if one may speak so) divine expedients for amelioration of evil, in which men and women may find divine work to do. As to the family and the church, — in each men fail of the ideal, but that does not impeach the institution as ordained of God. And some of us are bereft of the first; and there are some who never enter the second." Then, pausing, he added, " Much as I prize what I have seen to-day, I half wish I had not seen it."

Ralph's mother was not surprised at this view of the subject, nor at its vehement expression. It was like Ralph. She knew and sympathized with his earnest method of thought on all great subjects, and his sensitive manner of analyzing everything appealing to the sensibilities.

"Some such thoughts," she answered, " I suppose occur to every one who thinks at all. I had not taken such an extreme view of these cases. Or, if your view is not extreme, I had not thought so far."

But Mrs. Cushing's enthusiasm was not at all abated by Ralph's gloomy logic; and she went on with her own commentary in her own happy vein. And indeed, Ralph was himself quite as much interested, only taking the trouble to trouble himself with some passionate imagination of a contrast that never existed between his own childhood as it was and as it might have been. The very happy children whom he had that day seen for the most part did not know that there are such contrasts in the world, nor concern themselves at all that they might have been some thousands of times happier than they were. A few of the older ones had some vivid recollections of father and mother, (Oh, the mother!) and of home scenes too sweet to fade away. And these few, it must be owned, were the only ones of the many the light of whose happiness was toned with a shade that already gave their lives the beginnings of the strength of experience.

The conversation went on; they enjoying, the

while, the new scenes of the new road, and the glimpse of fair Kenyonville below.

The morning had brought letters from home; Mr. Cushing's to his wife being remarkably full of cheerful, homely details, and full, — as all his had been, — of the genuine admiration that was slowly moulding back again to the tender regard, and the appreciative, complacent love, so long hidden away; to come forth at last in the finer proportion of a ripe maturity. Rebekah's letter was addressed to Ralph, but it was really half to him and half to their mother. Brimming it was, and overflowing with sparkling gladness at the continued good accounts of "mamma's health," and at the deal of new, fresh enjoyment witnessed in the details given of their daily life. Cousin Cecilia's must be a charming family. And what a lovely region for country and climate! But the home-life at "Cushing Castle," as she gayly called it, since "intrenched" there with her papa and their faithful retainers, — Ralph must hear of that. There was always something new to give. It was really wonderful how well things went on, and how cheerful their father almost uniformly was. The house had not gone to ruin yet.

Such letters, received every few days, kept every homesick feeling at bay; and even made it seem almost real that they were themselves at home. Ralph was sure it was not the climate alone that was doing his mother good.

. . . .

They drove up to the Gray house just as Mrs. Stanley was ready to join them. She had made two delightful visits, she said; there was so much living, Christian faith in those households, with its consistent fruit of simplicity and neatness and industry. The great lesson always learned there was of our real oneness in Christ, and of our nearness to each other on that ground. When they reached home the visits were discussed further. The children always loved to speak of plain, sweet Nelly Brown. As for Ephraim, Mary did not " like " him very well. At least it was not agreeable to look at him. But she did think him very patient, and she noticed that his eyes followed Nelly everywhere. Frank thought him a fine fellow. He had been able to tell all about the books that Frank had lent him last, and they were always returned, Frank said, as perfectly nice as if they had not been opened."

" But old Mr. Gray," said Franky, " isn't he a delightful old man ? "

" *I* like him best of all," said Mary. " He has such a *bearing;* so somehow dignified and yet somehow humble. He has a pleasant way of meeting every one. And then, he converses as if he had brains and a soul."

" Oh, May ! " said Franky, " you are outrageous with your likes and dislikes ! "

" *I* like him," said Janie, " because he loves God, and has a pleasant voice. But all those people have pleasant voices, except Ephraim ; and I suppose he can't help the crack in his."

" Oh, Janie ! little Janie ! " cried Ralph. " Do

we like you because you are simple, or because you are funny?"

Janie did not know; but as Frank thought it must be because she was simple, Janie thought so too. "But since you love me," she said, "it is no matter *why.*"

CHAPTER XIII.

ATONEMENT.

RALPH'S mind had been busy with other thoughts than those touching the Orphan House. He had seen and heard much that afternoon that had condemned him, and that had raised again the question, ringing more loudly than ever, *What is truth?* "A real Pilate-question" he said to himself. "And if I do not receive Christ completely it is as if I sent him away to be crucified; for it is impossible to have nothing to do with Him."

The scripture-recitations had impressed Ralph

(252)

tenderly, deeply; but the singing of the hymn had not expressed the language of his heart. How could it? He was "recognizing, not believing." There was that in Christ that he needed. By his own confession he had long known and felt this, and that no one else could satisfy his sense of need, — his unrest. He even thought that he could not bear to hear that Holy One spoken against. Yet he was not laying his sins on Jesus. He was not fully satisfied that Jesus, whom he called " Lord," be *all;* and Ralph Cushing saved for nothing — *except* the mighty price that Jesus paid alone. There was within him an enmity toward God's chosen way of expressing to the universe His justice, unswerving and all lovely in its moral rectitude; an enmity against the demonstration of Calvary that the mercy of God (in which God delights) yields nothing of truth, and that the peace of God is not separated from a righteousness that is clean in His sight. The blood of Christ was not precious to Ralph; the putting away of sin by that means, and with no merit of ours, was not to his taste. There might be with God some higher, sweeter, more perfect judgment in this than is possible to any mere natural or human estimate Ralph was conscious of quailing under these re·flections. If God had spoken ; if God, all-wise, and infinite in goodness as in understanding, had spoken, it was man's business to listen, and to say, " Amen, O my God ! Blessed be thy name and Thy glory, and blessed be Thou in the hearts of Thy creatures; for Thou art God alone, and beside Thee there is no Saviour."

Ralph knew this; but he liked to place that IF before himself, for himself to stumble at. It seemed to make an excuse for his unsubmission to God's word, that was piercing him to the dividing asunder of soul and spirit.

Was Jesus then to be valued as the slain Lamb, who, in pouring out His soul unto death had borne the sins of many ? Or was the in·finite grace of that to be rejected ?

He remembered (he could not forget) Mrs.

Stanley's remark to him a few days before, — "When you get the view of Christ and of His work that God gives, your heart will be broken." He remembered the teacher's reply to Willie Jones, " God's judgments are *for* us, not against us, *if we are valuing the Redeemer's work and sacrifice as He does.*"

Ralph noticed that the two remarks fitted well together, and his soul rose up against their coincidence. For it showed him that he was surrounded by persons who were fully satisfied that tho things written of Jesus should be received as they are written ; that the declaration of an Atonement, one and sufficient, expresses the sovereign mind of the blessed God. He knew that these persons had what he had not, — namely, *peace.* And they seemed to have the Presence of a Person ; safety in a living Saviour. To him Christ was admirable ; he thought adorable ; but far off. To them Christ was the worshipped, the Beloved, the All-sufficient, the abiding One; *never* far off. Ralph knew that this was what he needed; and in some sense he *wanted* it. And he may have been right in supposing that he wished to accord to the Lord Jesus all His claims; to render Him all His due.

But this being saved for nothing, as regards ourselves, and saved by blood, — Ralph was not ready for this.

For it is not in human nature to submit to the righteousness of God.

During a conversation with his mother the same evening, Ralph gave some expression to these thoughts. And the responsive thoughts offered by her, spoken in great tenderness, kept faithfully before him that his state was simply one of rebellion against sovereign Redemption, against the written Word of God, which arrests the conscience with its own proof as being of God and not of man. "God could not give peace," she said, "until God's way of peace should be accepted. God's right hand has exalted Jesus, a *Prince* and a *Saviour*. He is as absolutely the one as the other, and He will not yield the right of being received. But," she added, "our dear cousin said too truly, my poor son. Your heart is not broken. It is still stout against this way of God's truth and grace."

"Have you not great anxiety about Cousin Ralph?" asked Mrs. Stanley, as the two ladies were sitting together, Ralph having gone up-stairs.

"Not *anxiety*," said Mrs. Cushing. "I have great *sorrow;* for he is not only not happy, but is, we know, *very wrong.* But I have no doubt that the work of God is underlying all this. Let him be in your prayers. That God is hearing us I do not doubt."

Mrs. Cushing had reason to speak thus. Without controversy, God's promise to the people of Jesus is that, if they honor Him before their ch'ldren, these shall not be forgotten before God. From their earliest days she had sought to impress her children with the truth as it is in Jesus, both by teaching and example. From the first, and without ceasing, there had been

17

prayer equally for them and for their father, in the belief that such prayer is according to God's will, and that in answering us He is but fulfilling His own gracious promise. The fact that neither Ralph nor his father were yet glad in God's salvation, did not shake her faith in God's promise, nor in His loving-kindness; but it opened her heart to a fuller learning of two needed lessons. First: that God, infinitely good, is sovereign still, and works when He will. And second, that there had been failures in her own faith and example which rendered it plain that this seeming delay on God's part conveyed a discipline altogeth r right, and for her profit. It never occurred to her to find any difficulty in harmonizing all this with the undoubted fact of Ralph's accountability for his own unbelief, and of God's waiting readiness to receive the heart's confession at any moment that it might be yielded. For the filial method of searching the deep things of God is as much above the controversial, as the heavens are above the earth,

God's way is a complete way, not patterned after any way of man. And the heart taught of God, and happy in its place of adoption, does not ask the head to analyze for it its consciousness of the truth of truth, and the love of love, and the light of the knowledge of God's glory in the face of Jesus Christ.

*   *   *   *   *   *

The next day the drive was, as had been planned, on the Nashville road, toward the Jamesons'. This was like "renewing old scenes," Ralph said. But the country between the Stanleys and the Jamesons looked differently now than on that moonlit night. The foliage was older, and more of it had fallen, and the dreamy sense of that bright, dim, half-penetrable lustre, was gone. What, then, is that strange, luminous essence which, by night, spreads both light and veil in one over the landscape, and stamps the mark of its impress on each subdued feature? allowing the pleased vision to see unsubstantially, -- multiplying shadows while it keeps darkness at bay ? It serves a purpose, but it makes no life, nor does it reveal anything in its true aspect. Let the light of day come in, and the charm is uncharmed, and the pretty thing vanished, — not being even missed. May there be some moral fact symbolical here that our dull senses fail to find ?

Rex was with the children to-day. Rex did not drive out often; having a fondness for home, and especially for the library, where he felt himself royal possessor, — although he set no value on the books, nor even knew there was anything fair either in look or love of those vine-clad shelves. If, in his regal state, he could have been lonely in the vacant library — his depopulated kingdom — all chance of that was lost in the company of Jack the canary, who sang to him the livelong time just for irrational joy at the absence of human creatures. But Rex had a long acquaintance with the Jamesons, whose estate he regarded as provincial to his own, and for whom he felt an interest half lordly, half affectionate. Thus it was that, hearing tho destination of to-day's drive declared, he (with a reflective self-possession that asks leave of no one) placed himself in the pony-carriage in ample season; the children, his loving subjects, seating themselves around him as best they might. Rex was always allowed to do as he liked when he essayed nothing wrong. Hence, when he chose to take a drive he was made quite welcome, especially by Frank and Janie. Mary had as lief he would stay at home; although, *when* at home, and in nobody's way, she confessed to liking him very well. But it was a matter of course, she said, that Rex should go with them when they went to the Jameson's.

And away they went at a round pace. Prince, the pony, who was growing old, had improved greatly since Penn and Philip had taken the lead. There was a spark of enthusiasm, and a whole fire of equine ambition, remaining in the stocky little animal yet; and his old, tired limbs, that used to be so nimble, were supple and young again under the stimulus of instinctive energy at the bare idea of being out-done. If he could have spoken he would have said, " You ought to have seen, you big young fellows, what I could do once." But there was something better than this in Prince after all. If he had a weakness regarding his own reputa-tion, he had also a high regard for the society of his own species; and would leap a hedge any day for the sake of grazing in horse company. Hence, the incoming of his new acquaintances to share his stable had been counted no intru-sion. It was nothing to him whether they ate of his grain or their own. He was younger in the stable, as well as on the road, because no longer enjoying his declining days alone. It would be a mournful day for the rejuvenated Prince when Penn and Philip should leave him.

．　　　．　　　．　　　．　　　．　　　．　，　　．

When the two carriages entered the enclosure bounding the homestead of which the white house was heart and centre, Ralph's curiosity, which had taken a comical turn from the start, sobered a degree or two. He began to think of the introduction to the lady dwelling there as a matter of polite fact; and of the meeting with the young preacher less as a matter of curiosity than as a matter of study, and one that might prove of more than passing interest. The house, too, in the midst of its modest and tasteful surroundings, looked less romantic and more dignified than in the moonlight of that night of long ago. Everything in the aspect of the place appealed more to respect than to curiosity. Ralph Cushing was not of a temperament in which superstition has any place. But he was possessed of a certain sobriety inherent to some deep natures; full of healthful, manly freshness that can abruptly, and without shock or affectation, take the place of a mirthful mood (so good and necessary in itself) whenever the real is best realized. This sobriety of which we speak, sweet and becoming where it flourishes most, is about as far from solemnity in any proper sense, as the verdured Highlands are from the peaks of Teneriffe or of the Jura. The one is within the reach and compass and understanding of every manly soul; the other is incomprehensible, and touched only by the few. The one is within happy access of any flight stronger than a butterfly's; the other is inaccessible except under some great impulse that we call divine. If Ralph was sobered when he entered the premises of these strangers, soon to be friends, it was simply that his strongest, manliest, truest side was outermost.

Zed rang the bell, with Mrs. Stanley's card announcing her friends. The door was opened by Alice, who retired with her usual well-meaning infelicity. But Mrs. Jameson would have no ceremony. She came out at once, not waiting for them to alight, overflowing with warm, decorous greetings. Graceful, simple, cordial, self-possessed, not overlooking the children, and filling all with a serene sense of welcome; she waited upon them in with a genuine dignity of which she had no need to be conscious, and which disturbed no one, because it belonged entirely to its possessor, and moved in a sweetness that seemed part of itself. Entering, they met Alice who had advanced as far as the hall. She was glad to see Mrs. Stanley, glad to see the children, and no one could see whether she was glad to see their two friends or not.

They were seated in the south parlor where everything, though inexpensive, bespoke the refinement that ruled the house. In answer to inquiries for Frederick, Mrs. Jameson said that he was in one of the orchards and would be disappointed not to see them. They must allow her to send for him. But Alice, fortunately if not handsomely, reminded her mother that there was no one to send; since the only servant "Jim," was gathering the fruit, whereupon Franky begged to be allowed to bear Mrs. Jameson's message, "and in that way he would have just what he coveted; the first greeting with Fred."

" My dear boy, yes indeed," said Mrs Jameson. " With your mamma's permission I would have sent a note by the driver. But you shall have your wish, and the note need not be written."

And Franky soon brought Frederick, who did not look ill in his russet suit of working clothes. His clear brown eyes and frank ease of manner were ornaments that he never examined, and could never put off. They were quite suffi- cient, and by their means alone he was well introduced everywhere. He might be the preacher; he might well enough be anything else honest and good.

Between these two young men an acquain- tance was not long in forming. There are cer- tain spiritual affinities that may find analogies in the laboratory, certain natures that draw out certain others, — or that are drawn into each other, neither being the stronger. Of these affinities, the physical are not a whit better un- derstood than the spiritual. In each case alike, the facts that we recognize, we acquiesce in; that is all.

Mrs. Stanley and Mrs. Jameson saw each other too seldom to make short visits possible. There was too much to say. Indeed, neither the Jamesons nor their guests were persons with whom conversation could flag ; nor was there likely to be much note taken of time. Mrs Jameson had taken Ralph from Frederick, and Frederick had turned to the ladies. Franky and Mary were absorbed in listening to the old folks, and Alice Jameson was entertaining Janie,— her only pet in the wide world except her brother Robert. Ralph had been much interested in Frederick's account of the way in which the homestead had been kept up since his father died; of the success of the vineyards and orchards ; of the sales of the fruits in Nashville, and of the happy hours spent at his cabinet-work, for which he had as many orders as he could well fill. Ralph making some reference to this when speaking with Mrs. Jameson of horticulture North and South, the lady gave expression to some happy thought as to " our Heavenly

Father's care and abundant blessing." Such thoughts were always uppermost with Mrs. Jameson, and their expression was as natural and genuine as it was inevitable, because the thoughts were so abundantly in the heart. The conversation flowing out of this remark showed Mrs. Jameson to Ralph as another of those enviable persons by whom he seemed surrounded of late, who, holding fast the letter of the Scriptures, were yet at rest as no one else seemed to be. And it showed Ralph to Mrs. Jameson as a lovely young admirer of Christ, who was well conscious of lacking something yet. This consciousness he defined for her himself. "It is," he said, "a consciousness of not possessing and being possessed by Christ. At least I conclude that is it."

Mrs. Jameson was not an inquisitor. She manifested her interest in her young friend's difficulties by a close attention to what he was disposed to say, and by such responses or remarks as might lead him to examine the Word of God more attentively, and to give it his whole confidence. "If you are settled," she said, "that the Bible affords its own evidence of Divine authorship, then you will find something there to rest upon, and God's way of peace, as declared in it, is surely not submitted for man's criticism, but for his acceptance."

Already, when defining his own position, Ralph had cited a verse from the Epistle of John (whose character, by-the-by, as a "son of thunder" is, throughout his epistles, remark-ably interwoven with the loving and beloved). The verse* was given by Ralph in candid avowal of his own condition as one of darkness. "For," he said, "*fellowship* must express a living, con-scious state between living persons. If I should profess to such relationship to Christ as that word expresses for all living Christians, I should simply *lie ;* nothing less or more." Ralph could now and then quote a verse from the Bible as expressing a real Divine truth, to be in no wise

* 1st John, i, 6.

doubted, yet would stumble at something in the immediate context. As if God would have given us a written embodiment of truth so lame, so sick, and out of joint in all its pages as to require every art of human logic to prop it up. In this case he had forgotten the verse following, to which Mrs. Jameson afterward called his attention: "But if we walk in the light as He is in the light, we have fellowship one with another, and the blood of Jesus Christ, His Son, cleanseth us from all sin." "To walk in the light," she said, "must be to let God's whole word shine upon us, and direct us. As the Lord Jesus Himself said, ' My mother and my brethren are those which hear the word of God and do it.' "

" But," said Ralph, " did they of whom that was said know anything about the doctrine of atonement as it is now declared, — by the blood of Christ? "

" Our Saviour Himself uttered many declarations concerning His blood and His sacrifice," said Mrs. Jameson. "The doctrine was perhaps less clearly stated then than afterward. We can receive or reject only what is presented. But we *are* made responsible to receive *what is* presented. The Lord just there, on the occasion referred to, had been enjoining them: 'Take heed how ye hear.' 'Unto you that hear shall more be given.' And that there was 'nothing secret that should not be made manifest.' "*

It was near this point in their conversation that Mrs. Jameson's attention was called by Mrs. Stanley, who desired her to hear some statements of her cousin's concerning certain charitable institutions at the North. Frederick, who had overheard his mother's last words with Ralph, gave her his chair, and, sitting again by Ralph just as he had been seated when speaking of the vineyards and cotton-fields, he said with the same frank manner and manly cheer, "Our faith does not stand in the wisdom of men, but in the power of God. We speak as the Word

* Luke viii.—Mark iv.

of God speaks, of 'being justified freely by His grace through the redemption that is in Christ Jesus, whom God hath set forth to be a propitiation through faith in His blood; . . . to declare at this time His righteousness: that He might be just and the justifier of him that believeth in Jesus."

There was power in those words. Ralph felt it. And they were sweetly, strongly spoken. Was it the words, or was it their enunciation, that seemed like shafts of light? He would so much prefer to hear more than to answer, that he bowed and made no reply. Frederick continued: "Such words are, *to them that perish,* foolishness. Nevertheless this Jesus, the Lord from heaven, was delivered for our offences and raised again for our justification. This is the testimony. It is God's testimony. He has given to us eternal life, and this life is in His Son."

"That is not disputed," said Ralph. "I dare say the life is in some way in Christ. I feel that it must be. But there is another point in your theology where I fail to see any beauty, — that 'without shedding of blood is no remission.'"

It was not strange that a shade of pain passed quick across Frederick's face, nor that he leaned a moment with his brow supported by both hands and his face quite concealed. There was certainly no affectation in it. No one could have failed to see that some quick, sharp, deep necessity bowed down that head and kept it bowed. And when he raised it again to speak, the eye was mellowed and the voice tremulous, — one could not have told whether with anguish or tenderness.

" Mrs. Cushing," he said, " we preach not ourselves, but Christ Jesus the Lord. If we do not preach Christ crucified ; Christ the ransom ; Christ's death for the life of His people ; we are not preaching the Gospel of God. There must be *some* awful significance in the fact that the Son of the living God assumed a nature in which He could receive the wages of sin in His own person ; and that He *did* receive it. What then

18

does it signify ? Surely only that He was there in His people's place. The momentary taking, by Christ the Lord, of the wages due sin, has taken condemnation away from His believing people. The wages was by Him fully received. The law cannot be executed twice. Now as to the blood: the whole scriptures are full of the idea that the life is in the blood. Blood represents life. The shedding of blood is the taking of life. When the blood of Jesus was shed, His *life* was taken from the earth. But death, or the forfeiture of life, being the wages of sin, it was not possible that the Holy One of God should taste it for himself. He tasted it for us. In it He received the condemnation due His people ; for He suffered as the Infinite One, and brought in life in infinite measure. God, who delights in mercy, is now seen at once as the Just and the Justifier. We receive, we rejoice in, forgiveness ; but in God's perfect way, wherein He delivers and sanctifies those whom the law had condemned.

" There is nothing sound, then, in making any difficulty about faith in His blood, or being washed in His blood. To mock, as some do, at this Divinely revealed truth on the assumption that the doctrine represents God as bloodthirsty, proves only that sin in us is blind to His grace and mad against it. (All such sin is surely of the same root as that which crucified Him once.) For it is to the praise of *the glory of His grace* that He has made us accepted in the Beloved ; in whom we have redemption *through His blood*, the forgiveness of sins, *according to the riches of His grace.* God being holy, and sin being exceeding sinful, how shall any dare to count as an unholy thing, or valueless, that blood of the covenant of redemption wherewith, in God's perfect way, the sinner's pardon is sealed ? "

And as Ralph again simply bowed, Frederick continued, —

" Indeed, I cannot understand, if you regard Jesus as the Son of God, the Lord from heaven, how you can see any meaning in His death, any explanation of it but *redemption, atonement,* the bringing in of eternal life to all those not rejecting it."

He paused. He had spoken calmly, tenderly, in no heat of controversy ; but earnestly, with quick, decided utterance ; as a man must speak who is speaking what he knows and testifying what he has seen, the issues being life or death only.

Ralph replied, " You speak convincingly ; and I may say that I have not before considered all this as fully as you here present it."

" Mr. Cushing," continued Frederick, " I must be safe in saying that you are not holding to the eternal Godhead of Christ, the Creatorship of the Redeemer. This is not to you the truth of all truth ; the heart's most precious conviction."

" You are partly right," said Ralph. " The impression that Christ is more than human, that He is in some sense Divine, is with me more than acquiescence in a theological dogma. I have held it as a moral fact of great value to our race, the full significance of which I have been conscious of not grasping. I have felt that there is that in Christ, as a living person, which I want and cannot rest without. But there are Scripture expressions with regard to His Godhead which I own are not held and cherished as convictions."

" No, surely not " said Frederick. " When it is so, you will be worshipping Him; at peace in Him; and His blood will be precious to you, — the cleansing blood. For it is as true now as it was in apostolic days, that ' whosoever believeth that Jesus is the Christ *is born of God;*' and ' whosoever shall confess that Jesus is the Son of God, God dwelleth in him and he in God.'"

" The mere confession does not cost much now-a-days," said Ralph; " and hence it seems to me no test."

"No," replied Frederick, "in the good ordering of God the mere avowal of one's self as a believer in Jesus, is not now-a-days at great

cost, — in general. But a genuine confession is
more than a mere *saying* so. The heart's confession of that living truth is always the work of
the Holy Spirit; for flesh and blood does not
reveal it nor make it precious. Let the heart
once be in possession of the truth as it is in
Jesus, and the confession of it becomes as
necessary to the individual as it is to the glory
of redemption. The heart's belief is attested
by confession. But, *as toward man*, the quality
of the confession is attested by the fruit that
follows; whether of endurance under persecution, or of love, gentleness, temperance, while
surrounded by evil. For when the Son of God
gave Himself for us, it was that He might redeem us from all iniquity, and purify unto Himself a peculiar people zealous of good works."

"I do feel," said Ralph, "that it would be
good to hold all these matters as assuredly as
you do. But I still have to say that I do not.
And as to good works, I know very well that I
have seen many persons zealous about them who

acknowledged no need of a Saviour. I never could feel in sympathy with those mortals who are quite satisfied with their own lives. But there *is* something not consonant with any degree of self-complacence, in this idea of salvation for nothing; life unmerited."

"Ah! But what have we to do with self complacence in such a matter as this?" asked Frederick. "It is indeed nature's way. But refine it to any degree you may, it is extinguished before the first glimpse of the Divine holiness. Human conceptions here are so low that humanity measures the Infinite by itself. As to good works again; there are none until we have life in Christ, — standing saved, complete in Him. Here again the human scale seeks to measure the Divine, and fails. But when, in that eternal bond-service — sweet as absolute — in which the Lord holds His dear people, our conscience is purged from dead works (no more law-working to get life) then, in Him, begin "good" works; for Thou O Lord hast wrought all our works in us.* This brings us to the blood-shedding again. The blood of Christ, who through the eternal Spirit offered Himself without spot unto God, can purge our conscience from *dead* works *to serve the living God.*† For the Way, the Truth, and the Life are in Jesus our Lord, who was delivered for our justification. To as many as received Him to them gave He the right to become the children of God; even to them that believe on His name. It is not a *getting*, it is a *receiving* with which we are concerned."

Rebekah's words exactly. Ralph recalled them with a strange emotion. He was too much interested to be wearied, and too much convinced to dispute. In this state he did not know what to say. Conscious of being convinced but not satisfied, he said what his reason was prone to fall back upon; though he might doubtless have said something that would have given his friend less pain.

<hr>

* Hebrews ix : 14.　　　† Isaiah xxvi : 12.

"Human nature," he said, "is quite likely much the same through all its contrasts. I hear some urging that they are not *good enough* to be Christians. I believe that after all, these stand very nearly where I do. To me there is something unwelcome in the idea of being good for nothing; able to do nothing but to receive; absolutely fit for nothing before God but to be forgiven."

"Nevertheless," said Frederick sadly, as the ladies rose to go. "Nevertheless we preach Christ crucified; to the self-righteous a stumbling-block, and to the learned foolishness. Life freely in Jesus. Life only in Jesus. Jesus crucified. Jesus risen. Jesus reigning. Jesus the beginning and the end. Happy are they who are not offended in Him."

.   .   .   .

And so the two parted; Frederick with his mother accepting an invitation from Mrs. Stanley to drive with her the next week.

The drive home was full of conversation in

harmony with all that they had seen and heard. Robert Jameson had come in from school toward the last of their stay; and, being quite jubilant at finding Mrs. Stanley there, had devoted himself to her; and had delighted Mrs. Cushing with his reminiscences of the last time he had seen the Stanleys; and edified her alike with some account of pretty Kenyonville, and with his unofficious attentions to his mother, — half boyish, half chivalrous, as they were. The ladies had had a good deal to say about the need of better institutions for the aid and education of the poor, both North and South; Mrs. Stanley being chiefly concerned as to the method, consistent with existing evils, of benefiting the black race.

"If we read prayers with our servants every morning," she said, "and give them a Bible verse or two, with some short Bible lessons on Sunday, we must not think it can be in vain, since it is of the grace and truth of God. But there is something wrong, *wrong* in the way their minds are kept down on a plane where there is no thought possible. I felt this more in other days, when I had more servants. Teach them to read! to think! Who dares to do it under this precious rule? I am not an abolitionist, but I *am* an *elevationist.* May the Lord save these poor people!"

So Mrs. Stanley had been feeling, and so she had been praying for many years. Mrs. Jameson sympathized with her, but did not altogether *think* with her. "Since the evil exists beyond our remedying," she said, "let us do the best we can with it. And let us at least admire the consistency of a State that refuses to enact educated slavery. If the colored race on this continent is liberated as a whole, — made self-dependent and entitled to citizenship, — *they will be educated.* But *moral* intelligence, certainly, is not dependent upon such a phase of *thinking* intelligence as is wrought out in what we term education. Independently of this — at least in a degree — the moral sense is developed and rectified in proportion as the conscience is instructed by the presentation of truth in language adapted to the hearers."

It was further added that when the heart is touched with God's love, the moral sense is always quickened and ready for instruction. The Stanleys' Richard and the Jamesons' Jim were cases proving this.

So these two ladies agreed, and so they differed. The theme arose again in the carriage, but Ralph heard less than usual, and asked fewer questions. Was he to be blamed if he was unwontedly silent? For eighteen centuries the minds of nations of men had been agitated about Jesus the Christ. The advance of nations in all the useful arts and amenities of life, could be clearly traced to the intellectual and moral animus emanating from Him. The centre about which human thought had been moving, or the point of departure whence it had gone exploring, was this Person; this Human Life other than human; this stepping into earth of Him who was before Abraham. He had been the Elevator of the race, — the Saviour of all men. They could not reject the temporal benefit, though they might seek to refute it, and might wholly miss the eternal.

Such thoughts as these were passing in Ralph's mind. And they were followed by the reflection that he was himself thus involved in a personal indebtedness to Christ that he could neither deny nor cancel. "Everything I have in this life," he thought, "existence itself, with all its benefits, I receive from God. And I am content enough that it be so. I have never thought of assuming part of the credit, — of having merited existence or anything belonging to it. My present life is full of good things that flow from Christ having lived on the earth ; and this is satisfactory enough. But to receive all for the Now and the Hereafter as the fruit of a Ransom paid, — as a *gratuity!* Why is it that opposition comes in here? Life out of His death, at once and for nothing; why do I hate this? Or do I not hate it?"

Ralph's mother and Mrs. Stanley of course noticed that his thoughts were busy, for it was not his way with them to listen and say nothing. He therefore was not listening. Mrs. Stanley presently asked him how he liked Frederick Jameson.

" Like him ? " exclaimed Ralph. " As I must like any admirable young man who can be pious without moping, and talk religion without drawling; and keep one talking or listening for five consecutive hours without either manifesting or inducing the slightest weariness."

" Five hours! Cousin Ralph. Our whole visit was one hour and a half."

" Oh, yes, very likely. I mean that he might have talked on for five hours without getting to the end. I like him all over and altogether; only I have not made up my mind to agree with him."

Ralph had assumed his reckless manner, which his mother well knew was an affectation indicating that he would rather not pursue the subject, and she drew Mrs. Stanley's attention another way. Presently Ralph asked his mother if she made the acquaintance of Miss Alice.

" Yes," said Mrs. Cushing, " I found her quite approachable and intelligent, and, as Mary would say, or should say, *likeable.* But she was not much near us. Janie and Frank absorbed her mostly. Mary, be it noticed, was very agreeable to her."

" Mary is a real comfort to me," said Mrs. Stanley. " She knows how to receive an admonition. And she does love her mother."

And Mrs. Stanley's eye lighted with a joy that it is neither in wealth nor in station to give, nor in any success. Nor does it come of any possession save that of the loving subjection of a beloved child.

" Yes, she is a dear girl, truly," said Mrs. Cushing. " You have a deal of comfort in all your children."

" Janie is remarkable," said Ralph, so bluntly that the others could not tell what he meant. But Mrs. Stanley took alarm.

" Oh! Janie has many faults," she said, " and is not precocious in gifts. She learned to read early, and is beginning to *think* early; but she has all the troubles of any other child, and is as fond of a romp as of a book."

" As for Franky," said Mrs. Cushing, " he is ready to quarrel with Ralph for appropriating Mr. Jameson ' *the whole time*,' as he says."

" Oh, I'll risk Frank on a quarrel," said Ralph, more gayly than he had spoken before ; adding, " What is it that makes that family so charming ? "

" It is love," said Mrs. Stanley, " just love ; *love in the light.* Their living faith strengthens the natural ties a thousand-fold. It is not often that one sees an entire family so completely of one heart and one mind in the truth."

.   .   .   .

Three days followed, during which Sunday intervened, and on the other days rain prevented the usual drive. Ralph was not sorry for this, except on his mother's account, to whom the drives were certainly a benefit. For himself he was glad to have his time less interrupted just now. Study and thought were pressing him. Except during the morning hours, which were devoted to his law-books, he was roaming over the book-shelves or making himself useful to his mother and agreeable to everybody. What he liked best of all, except doing a real service to some one, was a frolic with Janie; sometimes lively, sometimes of a very intellectual sort, as when he reclined on the lounge and she would sit near tangling his hair and exchanging her bright thoughts for some of his, or asking questions that he could sometimes answer and sometimes could not. On the Sunday he had been much arrested by a sermon from Mrs. Stanley's minister, drawn from the words: "Though we have known Christ after the flesh, yet now henceforth know we him no more. Therefore, if any man be in Christ he is a new creature." He saw that, at best, his knowledge of Christ hitherto had been after the flesh. Christ admirable, wonderful, adorable, but still Christ as He walked the earth in lowliness, in humiliation, under a veil of flesh and blood, had been the Christ of his contemplation; not Christ risen, the Man triumphant, the Lord of glory, in the glory also that He had with the Father before the world was; the Almighty, the Prince and the Saviour.

Ralph's thoughts with the Bible were deeper and more tender after this. Nothing concerning Christ could be lightly treated. He must be *in* Him in that new creation.

With the exhortations to those already confessing Christ, which closed the sermon, he felt that he had at present less to do.

"Dear brethren," said the preacher, "if we live in the Spirit, let us also walk in the Spirit. Beware that you do not dream of being in Christ while you are covetous, or provoking and envying one another, or absorbed in fashion, setting your hearts more on the newspaper and the world's progress than on the word of Christ and the progress of His truth. These things are of the old creature; not of the Father but of the world. Oh, my brothers! if the word of Christ is not dwelling in you richly, how is it that you are new creatures in Him?"

It was towards evening of the next day that Ralph, after a letter to his father (glowing with details of their daily existence, of the dear mother's health, and of the good, stupid law-studies,) had brought a book from the library to the parlor where his mother and her cousin were sitting; the library being given up to the children, who were making themselves wild over their sister Gracie's accounts of the Yosemite Valley. The book had caught his eye in the morning as he was searching for some old law-book of Mr. Stanley's. It was a volume of dis-courses in the French, entitled *The Redeemer.** He sat for some time reading, for the language was attractive, the thoughts singularly strong

* Le Redemption : per Edmond de Pressense.

and devotional, the theme in harmony with Ralph's mood. The pages with the reading of which he closed the book contained the following words:—

" Fasten your eyes upon that cross, my brothers, and turn then from it no more. That it is that consummates your redemption. All the sufferings that constitute condemnation are gathered up in that immolation. Enclosed and accepted in an act of complete obedience, accepted by the Just and the Holy, and consequently turned into saving expiation. . . . Shall I speak of the agonies of the soul, of that cry, ' My God ! My God ! why hast Thou forsaken me ?' What mysterious link between condemned humanity and the only Son of the Father does that astonishing word reveal, which no human explanation would know how to interpret ! Shall I speak of the sorrow which sums up and confounds all others, — of that which is the essential wages of sin, namely, of *death ?* What prodigy may equal this, that the Prince of life has died ? . . .

That wages of sin He has received, He, the sinless. . . . If it be true that all the griefs of human life have fallen upon that sinless head; if He for it has made one alone sacrifice, and if He has offered it to His Father in his liberty and in His holiness; then recognize with Him that there is nothing more to do for salvation; for there is nothing more to suffer, nothing more to accept; and say with Him, It is finished."

While Ralph had been reading, Mrs. Stanley had left the room, and, as he closed the book, he found himself alone with his mother. He told her, more freely than he had yet found opportunity to do, of his conversation with Frederick Jameson, and of the still further thought awakened by the sermon he had since heard.

"If it be true," he said, "that Christ has become a High Priest of good things to come, and has by His own blood entered in once into the holy place, having *obtained eternal redemption for us;* if all this be so, it is a solemn pity indeed to be finding any fault with it. But pride (if it be pride), is in the way, — fearfully in the way with me. I am not accepting the idea of *self* being nothing, and good for nothing, — just worth nothing at all."

" We are nothing, and good for nothing, surely," said his mother, " as to any strength or excellence. But we are not *worth* nothing. We are worth so much to God that He has made a way to save us, — a way to bring us into His presence with exceeding joy."

" You take up my words in metaphysical earnest," said Ralph. "I dare say you are quite right, that in the spiritual sense there is a difference between good for nothing and worth nothing."

" It is not strange, my dear son," continued Mrs. Cushing, "if no flesh may glory before God. Since He has chosen to provide for the unrighteous a righteousness that can stand in His sight, and a redemption that can put away sin, and in the end deliver from it; and since in so doing He has made a way to win our love, let us not think that we are worth nothing to Him; let us acknowledge, as is fit, that the *worth* is not *merit;* that as to goodness we are indeed nothing; and, indeed, accord all to Christ, since we have all in Him. It is God's infinite power and equal grace that place the Christian so completely in Christ that he stands no more before God forever. Christ is become the wisdom, the righteousness, the sanctification, as He is the redemption. Now if we glory, we glory in Him, the Lord, the Saviour. It is enough, surely, that He be honored in what He has wrought. Oh, Ralph, dear Ralph! the *will*, the *pride;* when will they be broken in you? Ralph Cushing will not be nothing — no, not even that Christ may be all! But of course Ralph Cushing is quite impotent to change the blessed, eternal fact that Christ *is* all."

Ralph remembered Rebekah's words: "Submission is happiness when it is a right submission." He was silent a moment, and then only said, "The right of Nicodemus! How can these things be?"

And as Mrs. Stanley entered just here, he addressed her with his quick politeness, that she might not feel herself intruding. "Mother and I are on the theme that you know is all-absorbing just now, and with which I know you are in sympathy."

"Yes, indeed I am," she answered, with sweet, hearty emphasis.

"But mother has talked as long as is good for her," he continued, "and I am going (you will excuse me) to put away my book, but not your kindness nor my thoughts."

And as he entered the library he found Janie alone ; even Rex gone. Richard had opened the door, Janie said, with the intelligence that Susan was in a heap of trouble about something ; and would Miss Grace please, go see ? " Mary had gone with Grace, and Frank had gone off somewhere with Rex. So only Janie was left, too intent upon some sampler-work to be disturbed by the desertion.

"Ah, well Janie ! this is just right," said

Ralph as he put up his book. "My head needs stroking sadly. So I will go down on the lounge and your sampler shall go into the basket, and you will sit by me."

"Yes indeed, Cousin Ralph" said Janie, ever ready to do what was asked.

She drew up her chair, and her tiny fingers parted his locks and wandered over his temples with a marvellous effect on the ache that was there, and the weariness. Almost always at such times she chatted loquaciously, or asked questions and waited for answers. But now she was intuitively aware of his mood; and, in more sympathy than understanding, kept silent.

"Well Janie?" said Ralph, after the rest had passed from her finger-tips softly, sweetly, deeply, through and through the brain that had been so sore a few minutes ago. And, as she did not respond, he opened his eyes toward hers and repeated, "Well Janie?"

"Cousin Ralph," said the child, "the Lord Jesus is the good Shepherd, and His sheep hear

His voice. Perhaps you are not one of His sheep."

Ralph was taken by surprise. Was he awake or dreaming? How could this child know what he was thinking of?

He only weighed her words, and said again, " Well Janie? "

The poor little voice faltered as she proceeded, " But I wish you were. I wish you would be, *now.*" The little head was bowed only a moment. Then she lifted it up.

" Well Janie, I am listening." Ralph forced himself to speak firmly.

The child gathered up her voice again, and spoke strongly now. " Well, then, He laid down His life for the sheep. And they follow Him."

She paused again; and the pause grew so long, so very silent, that Ralph again spoke.

" Janie, what would you do if you were me ? "

" Cousin Ralph," she said, " I think I would

take the cup that Jesus filled with His salvation.
There it is, full, and held out for you; and
so good! Why don't you drink it?"

.   .   .   .

Oh, Ralph! Ralph Cushing! It is well for
you that you could lie there no longer.

.   .   .   .

He rose up, but he did not at once stand upright. He sat a moment with his brow on his
hand, as one not knowing what had happened to
him. It was as if transformation had passed
upon all things. Yet he was a real man, in a
real world. And the child was there by him;
a real child, not an angel. He knew this. And
then he knew he must cry out something that
even she might not hear. He must be alone
with the Unseen. He must go. But he would
not go in silence. He would not leave the
ministering child joyless. He stood upright
now. He bent down over her.

"Janie! Why Janie!"

And his tone was so changed that she knew

what he meant. And then he went out: and Janie settled back to her needle-work, happy because knowing that Ralph was happier, but not at all understanding what a stupendous work God had wrought by her means.

And where could Ralph go but to his own room? For he had a friend now whom he wished to meet there. We have no business with what he said to that Friend, nor with what that Friend said to him. The only words uttered that we are permitted to record were such as have been uttered by many a soul before, and by many a one since.

"O Jesus, Saviour! my Lord, my God! How art Thou become precious!"

CHAPTER XIV.

HOME CORRESPONDENCE.

T was about this time that Ralph wrote Rebekah as follows : —

"STANLEY MANSION,
November 10th, 18—.

" DEAREST SISTER : —

With whom do I compare you? Since 'dearest' denotes comparison in a degree superlative, you cannot be the dearest by virtue of being the only sister I possess. In this style of address I claim that you are the dearest sister alive. This is not claiming to be acquainted

with everybody's sister. It is only the assuming
that you have as strong a place in fraternal affection as it is possible for a sister to have; and
therefore, doubtless, you stand with few **fears** in
that regard, if you be not queen of all.

"So many things to write you to-day! although I wrote only four days ago, and mamma
has written in the meantime. I do not know
how to classify the news and the chat I have to
give. It is not at all certain that I shall begin
with the least, but I shall end with the greatest.
So proceed patiently with one.

"And first, *not* least. Mamma is improving so
much, the climate is evidently so well suited to
her, and the autumn is proving so unusually
mild, that we are content to prolong our stay
here beyond our first intent. This, of course, is
at Mrs. Stanley's invitation and, indeed. urgency. She declares that nothing has enriched
her life so much, for years, as our coming and
our remaining; and, so far as mother is concerned, this may well be true. If the winter

continues quite moderate we may remain even into the new year. In that case we should abandon the project of proceeding southward in our own carriage; but, pushing westward to Memphis, take steamboat passage South, carriage and all; unless, indeed, we send Zed and the equipage back to you. Louisiana seems very far away, and the going there more like a desertion of home — or of the loved ones that *make* home — than the remaining here. For Tennessee, on the map, looks much nearer, and, practically, might prove so if all were not well with you at any time. Nothing but the duty of carrying out, if possible, what we have undertaken could induce either of us to increase the distance of separation, or even to prolong the stay into all the allotted months. How long they must seem to you! But you have your own sweet perversity about not coming to take my place. And indeed, on father's account, you are quite right; since I could not fill for him the place that you are filling. You make his house cheerful, and keep the servants in order; and your presence is doubtless all that enables him to bear so kindly mamma's absence. And then your little 'sewing circles' of rich children for the poor, and of poor children for missionaries. What an original invention! I surely could not carry those on for you. We were much interested in your account of them.

"It is some time since I have written you specially about the law studies. They progress doggedly. Indeed, no—I will take that back,—they progress quite cheerily on the whole; with more interest than I had supposed could accrue in my own case. Since we now anticipate remaining here so long, I have entered my name as law student in the office of Judge Hazelton, Mariondale. This will give me free access to his fine library, and seems more like work in earnest than the method pursued thus far. This, also, will bring me in contact with 'cases' in counsel; and if we are here until the second week in January, when court sits, I shall see *how they do it.* "Still, still as of old, — I don't like it. Can I *ever* like it?

"Cousin Gracie, as she is pleased to be called, has returned from her prolonged visit in Cali·· fornia; accompanied by Miss Penelope Clayton. (You have heard of our neighbors the Claytons. ' Neighborhoods ' here have an extent elsewhere unknown.) The fair cousin is of the invalid order in theory only ; having a robustness that it must require courage on the part of a physician to pronounce against. After almost a year in that Golden State, whose capital is practically farther from Washington than Montreal is from London, she returns with quite a provincial air, which young people are prone to acquire or to affect. But the young lady is a Stanley every way. Miss Clayton turned aside to dine with us before going on to her brother's; the vehicle passing this way. I should pronounce her one of those sincere well-bred individuals whose genuine worth is manifest to all but themselves and the sorry few who lack all discernment.

20

" I believe you have not yet been told of our introduction to the Jamesons. We took a pleasant afternoon for a drive that way, and found them not only ' delightful ' (which word, like other rapturous adjectives, is getting quite too common) but a *remarkable* family I judge them to be. Frederick, the young man of whom I once wrote, who works lustily all the week, and is said to preach lustily on Sundays, is certainly no ordinary youth ; albeit, his gifts are doubtless from God who called him. The respect and attraction that I felt for this new acquaintance, whose amiability is equal to his strength, have grown or passed into genuine affection, — nay *love* — (for why not use the simpler, greater word ?) since I realize how dear he must be to the Saviour who is now, only *now*, dear to His poor servant, Ralph Cushing.

" For, my own only sister, I felt that I must keep the greatest news for these last pages, since with no other theme could I finish a letter to you just now. The light broke in, the heart melted, the will ceased from itself, under some words from that sweet child, Janie, whom the Lord has assuredly called. Oh, Rebekah! what a fool I have been, what a proud creature! I can fling no worse reproach over my past self than these words,— *a proud creature.* Nothing could be worse. Pride in the human heart before God! Objections before God! Strictness upon the wisdom, the perfect way, of God! narrowing down the broad commandment, assuming a dictatorship as to Divine ways and means! Not touching the hem of Christ's garment, out of a humiliation and a need that must draw from the Lord of all; but, with the foot of pride, *stepping upon it!* Rebekah, I remember your words; mother's words; Mr. Clearwater's manly, earnest preaching, and his personal entreaty so delicate always, and yet plain. I have had many good words also from Mrs. Stanley, and from others. And how is it that through all I have been *deaf, blind, dead?*

But, though thus it has been, this is not all. 1 *would not* see the Saviour, the *Saviour*, the *Lord.* Jesus was too exalted. Salvation was too free. Redemption by blood was not acceptable. The cup was there, filled with life, eternal life, held out to me by the Lord of Life; His own purchase, His own gift. And when that child spoke softly about this, and said, ' Why don't you drink it ? ' then, just then, God was pleased to show me what love I was rejecting, what rebellion I was hugging ; what a fool,—oh! *what a* fool I had been! And what a great Saviour, — present, living, all-sufficient, — the poor fool had now found.

" Shall I say any more ? Is it possible to say more ? I do not need to tell you that the truth of God is no longer a problem; nor that the worship of Jesus is the life of the soul. I do not need to tell you that the poor fool's folly is forgiven ; that the sinner's sins are washed away. You are rejoicing with me, for now at last we are worshipping one Redeemer.'·

This letter accompanied one from Mrs. Cushing to her husband from which the following brief extract is given : —

" Doubtless Ralph has written Rebekah of the change in his views and attitude regarding the Saviour.   It is, you must know, a great joy to me that Ralph's confession of Christ is at last clear and decided, and that the manly, restless heart has rest.   In this my joy you cannot, I am sure, withold a certain sympathy.   Give me all you can.

" Ralph is quite earnest in his studies, for your sake.   A good son we may both count him." . .

.   .   .   .

To these letters Rebekah replied as follows : —

" Home, November 14th, 18 —.
" Dear Mamma and Ralph : —
The news of all the year comes in your letters of the tenth received to-day.   I had to run away and weep for joy.   Oh, Ralph ! dear old brother, I knew it would be so.   You know

I said there would be a good end, — not because I believed *in you*, but because I was persuaded that God was breaking you to pieces. He was only letting your pride raise you very high, that you might fall on that stone on which it is good to be broken. There is no need to gather up the fragments of the broken heart, since a new heart is given. You are still Ralph, my very brother Ralph, though in Christ a new creature. How are old things passed away now?

" But I am writing to you both, — to mamma and Ralph! I cannot keep the tears from falling on the paper while I write; tears of joy, and of longing to see you. I am happy and well-occupied all day long; and quite content I assure you, *more* than content, to have things just as they are, especially since I realize more by each new letter received how good a thing it is that we sent you away, mamma. And God has made it work good for Ralph, too. No doubt He will overrule for us all that we commit to Him. I say this for Ralph's strengthening, or comfort or whatever of such words he prefers. The law-office entry was a good movement, papa thinks. You both do me good by your faithful letters, in which you make me share so well the daily life you lead.

"And this brings me to relate to you a few incidents that have transpired recently with us.

"I wrote you that Rose Bailey was quite sick; and now she has passed away — the sweet, fair Rose; the loving Rose. I had already been twice to see her, when, three evenings ago, a messenger came saying that she was suddenly failing, and 'begged to see Miss Cushing once more.' Papa said he would drive me himself, which was a great treat to me, — the more so that on an errand so sad I would need some one to speak to.

"Rose had been everything to her mother and sister, who are really broken by this loss. As for Rose herself, happy Rose (a 'rose-bud' I had always called her; a rose full-blown now), she seemed to have passed through more than a life-

time since I last saw her in health, only there
was nothing like *age.*   It was a ripeness without
decay, — a weary evening, glowing and fragrant,
and fading into a sweet sleep that awaits a sure
waking again.

" ' It is sweet,' she said, ' to think of being
so soon with Jesus in Paradise, — perhaps even
to-day.'

" And after we had talked a few minutes, —
she speaking very slowly and softly for weakness,
— she told me that there was one trouble, — a
temptation, a *something,* in her experience, which
did not disturb her peace; but still, to have it
gone would be a great joy. She was assured
of forgiveness, of acceptance in Jesus the Christ,
the Beloved. He was dear to her as *her* Saviour, *her* Lord, worshipped and rested in. But
could she know that His love was consciously,
individually, taking note of each, even the least,
and therefore of her ?

" I was very glad that Mr. Clearwater came in
just here. In answer to her question he said

decidedly *Yes;* but it is a matter for consciousness, not for logic. 'Let us pray,' he said. And after prayer, — a prayer of thanksgiving and praise, — a few words from Scripture were repeated, such as ' We love Him *because* He first loved us,' and 'He calleth His own sheep by name.'

" ' Yes, there it is,' said Rose, with the *great joy* in her eye. 'He does reveal Himself by His word. He does especially love each one of us. How gracious all this is ! '

" She passed away the next evening. It was a sinking, sinking, as if to sleep. Not in apathy (as when ' there are no bands in their death'), but in peace, because the Lord was there. ' It is so sweet,' she said, ' to know that the Lord went down among these shadows, and in His rising again gave us the assurance that it is all safe for His own beyond.'

" The meaning of the words ' Christ in you the hope of glory,' (exemplified in her sweet life for years), was, in her dying, marvellously manifest. Her words to her mother, that fell most sweetly into her old heart were, 'Mother, doesn't Jesus comfort you? He *will* comfort you.'

"In all the house there was peace.

"I must reserve incidents touching life at home for another letter."

.   .   .   .

A few days later Rebekah wrote as follows:
. . . "The best news touching the home estate is that Ethelred's patience is rewarded, and his particular sorrow is at an end. Faith came to see me the other day, and told me that her father had been so much in admiration of Ethel's conduct, that he was ' 'shamed,' (he said), 'of his own hardness in the matter.' 'Father overblames himself,' she continued, ' for thee knows it was for conscience sake he took the stand he did. But he now says Ethel is proved a noble fellow, controlled by the principles of the true Gospel. And that if he does not feel that he can enter the Society, that must not signify; for, to deny his suit, would be to darken two lives without cause.'

" And so they are to be married next month.
Ethelred is already opening and airing the cottage, and putting in one thing after another.
This morning, being the day for bringing flowers
to the house, I told Joan to keep him and call
me. I was with papa in the library ; and, at his
permission Joan got orders to send Ethel in. He
came through the hall whistling under breath.
(Good Ethel, for a strange thing, forgot his good
manners so far as that.) He is growing con-
templative, and, I dare say, whistles unconsciously. He brought the flowers, and recollected
himself with many humble apologies for his
carelessness in the hall. I told him that I almost envied him his calling ; at which he made
some candid reply, after the fashion of his own
simplicity ; declaring that it must be an ancient
calling, since " those that dwelt among plants
and hedges " are mentioned in the patriarchal
section of the Chronicles. Ethel's memory is
stored with Scripture, you know, which always
serves him well. I said to him that papa and I

must wish him joy of the good end of his waiting
— not so very long after all. And papa, being
somewhat complacent toward the affair, interposed some odd remark to the effect that Ethel's
Faith and Hope had not disappointed him. But
Ethel, standing decorously with hat in hand,
sobered a little at this, and begged Mr. Cushing's
pardon if he might take the remark in the
highest sense and protest that a Christian's faith
and hope cannot disappoint; being the gift of
God. 'And so is a faithful wife,' said papa.
Ethel did look satisfied ; and when I made an
errand with him to the hall window to show
him how the fuchias and begonias were thriving, he said to me, 'Doctor Laidley, ma'am,
says that faith toward God is not *gained*, it is
sovereignly *given*.' 'Yes Ethel,' I said, 'but
Doctor Laidley would say also that when men
seek God, He is found of them. Both statements
are true, I think. The prayer " What must *I do*
to be saved ? " is being answered every day.'

" Ethel looked as if he would speak if he

dared, and I encouraged him to go on. 'It remains ma'am,' he said, 'that there is one God the Father, of whom are all things . . and one Lord Jesus Christ, by whom are all things, and we by Him. Doctor Laidley would say, ma'am that God moves us to seek Him. Since He is all and over all, absolute, eternal, and infinite, His grace is so also.' 'Ah well, Ethel' I said, ' God gives us the breath we draw ; but *we draw it.*' 'Yes ma'am,' he answered, ' the breath and the drawing of breath ; we cannot separate the thing from the act. All is of God.'

"You see, mamma, Ethel is a monarchist in every sense ; more monarchical than analytical. I concluded the discussion (shall I call it so ?) by agreeing with him that we can do nothing without God — in a sense that divests us of all sovereignty, but not of responsibility. To whom could we be absolutely responsible but to an ab-solute Sovereign who works all things after the counsel of His own will ? Everything, to us, hinges upon doing what is bidden. The blind man cannot make his eyes see, but he can go to the pool and wash. Use God's means for finding God, and God will be found. The great means to this is the searching of His own word. 'Ah! yes ma'am,' he said, 'the entrance of His word giveth light. There are many sweet thoughts about our Father's Sovereignty. Doctor Laidley says we are to look at it filially. The good man gives us a wonderful deal to think of, ma'am. So much of the love of God to sinners; so much of His ways in Christ; so much *of Christ!* I said to him one day, ma'am, "Pastor Laidley, how is it that you can say so much that does us good; and always so easy; as if there was only to open the mouth, and the word o' wisdom flows out?" "Ah! Ethel," says he, "don't ye know it is naething to pump if ye hae a head o' water on?" And then he sighed, like, (he has a sweet way to sigh betimes,) and said, "But Ethel, my boy, we hae this treasure in earthen vessels, that the excellency o' the power may be of God, and not of us." '

"By-the-by, mamma, I had a call from Doctor Laidley the other day. He came in, sweet, and strong, and hearty as ever; with grace always flowing out of his lips, as Ethel says. He was glad to hear of your improvement, and sent some stately compliments to you. He also gave me the very best and most helpful sympathy touching your absence, that I have had from any source. He talked a long time of Christian love — a theme of which, you know, he never tires, — with his sweet, rich-sounding *Kreestyan* for 'Christian;' and much else in charming Scottish accent that I cannot imitate, either with tongue or pen. 'Under the light of the Cross,' he said, ' and in this dispensation of grace, full scope and opportunity are made for the exhibition of God's love. And His Spirit, who is in His children, leads them to love one another; as He says to them in His word, Little children love one another, for love is of God.'

"I confessed that I do not always feel affectionately towards certain ones who are undoubtedly Christians. He replied, ' You probably do feel so toward whatever of Christ you discern in them ; and a desire that His grace may be enlarged in them, as well as communicated to the perishing. But,' he added, 'Christian love is not merely a sentiment ; it is *a principle.* Indeed it is both, — *it is both.*'

" I was much delighted with his call; all the more Christian and neighborly because we are not of his parish. I am quite flattered that twice during the conversation he told me that I had ' made an excellent point.' Papa appreciated his visit very much.

" I give you these incidents at such length because I have the time to write, and I know you are glad not to have them passed by. Papa seemed much touched by what I told him of the scene in Rose Bailey's sick-room. But he said little."

.   .   .   .

Ralph had indeed been, as Rebekah said,

broken in pieces. He had been made so miser-
ably sensible of his own insufficiency to his own
need, that long before his heart yielded to the
truth, he knew that there was nothing possible
to himself but to yield ; and that there was no
way for a creature to glory before God. Vanity
was thus excluded while pride still held out.
The blind man whose eyes, it seemed, were
already anointed by the Lord of Glory, was halt-
ing about that simple, distasteful, washing in
the pool. Because, while pride still has place in
the creature, the Lord is not fully believed ; the
heart is not giving Him His due place as the
One who filleth all things, and who must therefore so fill the heart as to be the worshipped
One, the chief Beloved. When we are truly in
His company no idol can stand near us ; and in
fellowship with Him we walk in the light ; the
" desires of the mind " cease to be fulfilled.

But now, not only was the vanity cast down,
the pride also was broken ; the idols were abol-
ished. The Lord of all, while subduing whom

21

He will, yet waits to be received. And now being admitted to this broken heart; being held by the feet and worshipped; He took these native gifts, which at the first came from Him, and sanctified them, — brought them into holy service. Ralph Cushing, the forgiven sinner, that is, the Christian, was sitting a learner at the feet of Jesus. That large, ever-thinking intellect was illumined now to discern spiritual truths, and to think in the mind of Christ. It was first of all, as with one in ancient days, and with many a one since, — 'behold he prayeth!' And then such daily lessons of his own need were imparted, and daily such infirmities were manifest, that the sense of dependence grew, and the sweetness of the living bread and water were sought and found daily. Prayer in the Holy Spirit once begun could not cease. The Passover had been realized ; the forgiveness had been received ; and now the heavenly manna, and the water out of the rock were the soul's life. All this expresses fellowship ; fellowship with the Father, and with His Son Jesus Christ, which only the forgiven soul has, and in which Ralph daily grew, because by God's good hand kept so low that the Lord could raise him up.

Let none suppose that all this, in its genuineness, is given to those who put a self-complacent trust in "interior revelations" or an "inner light," — terms with which the devil dupes the simple and persuades them to be wiser than God. The Bread of Life is the Living Word, who is pleaded to reveal Himself to the true flock by means of the *word written*, and to meet the soul in *prayer uttered*. If any neglect these means, to which the Holy Spirit leads, let them not think that they are led of the Spirit.

.   .   .   .

Thus it was that, in the strength of this growth imparted, Ralph wrote Rebekah some things that follow : —

"December 2nd.

GOOD SISTER, WELL-BELOVED : —

"I have let mamma do most of the

writing of late, giving you only short notes; chiefly for the reason that Judge Hazelton's books and *cases* absorb most of my time, — time being a Divine trust that it becomes us to invest well. I have, however, written father once quite fully. . . . I like Doctor Laidley's thoughts on Christian love. It surely is not *the profession of religion* that makes Christians dear to one another. It is *Christ in us.* A heart that honors Christ is dear to his brother because dear to Christ; because Christ has set His love upon him and is bringing him to the glory.

" The youngest, the weakest, may be taught what *love* means; for all are ' taught of God to love one another.' But Divine *knowledge*, as Divine grace, is that in which we must *grow.* Sometimes I am so hungry and thirsty for more of Him who is ALL, that my soul faints in me. The precious things of Christ! the deep things of God! We cannot know all, nor set all that we may know in right order, until we see Him as He is. Beyond the foundation of our faith, of our peace, — the simple good news of life in Christ, — there is a progress of doctrine, or a progression in revealed truth, to be followed only by the renewed mind; only by him who is spiritual, — and in each case according to the prayer bestowed, according to the faith, according to the grace given. . . . . I shall, I dare say, find time to write you again soon, and a mood to give you more of incident. Of late the weather has been too cool for driving, but not for comfort in-doors with a light fire. Mamma's strength is so well advanced that she now walks out with pleasure, and thus avoids too close confinement. Should there be any check in her progress, we shall hasten on southward. We have two letters, within as many weeks, from the Farr cousins, urging us not to delay longer. Our attachments here are becoming so strong and so many that we shall regret to move in any direction except homeward. The Claytons, upon further acquaintance, are indeed admirable neighbors. Frederick Jameson, dear

Christian fellow that he is, was more sweetly moved than I had supposed it possible for a man to be, by my confession to him that in resisting his words I had resisted a message from God; and by my account of how the Lord had at last broken me and shown me Himself. It was at his own house that I told him this; for, although he was to drive here the next day I could not let him wait. It was on the day following,—that (to me) happy day of all,—that I borrowed the pony and rode over to see him. I found him at his work in the field, looking much the same as when we first met. And when he said, ' Oh, my brother! only the Lord can break the gates of brass, and He breaks them by whom He will.' I understood a little of what is meant by the joy in heaven over one sinner that repenteth. For the repentance is a change of mind toward God in His message of life.

" Frederick's brother Robert is a fine youth, but I think not equal to his mate Orpheus Clayton. But in some sense the fairest life of all here, the one from whom I learn the most, is this little Janie, who is, after all, a romping, glowing, hearty child, in no way morbid, and, if unusually intelligent, is at least healthfully so. Her leading characteristic is a quick, accurate conscientiousness.

" Our congratulations to Ethel, and greetings to all the servants. Mamma and I have thanked you much for your untiring details of home; and we are indebted to you for narrating the last scenes in Rose's life. Her poor mother, and Amelia! How are they off this winter for the comforts of life? I need not remind you to be beforehand with them. They are slow to acknowledge a need of that kind. . .

RALPH."

CHAPTER XV.

PLEASANT CONVERSATION.

ONE Saturday, the young people from Clayton Hall having dined at Mrs. Stanley's, Fred and Rob Jameson came in. Herbert Clayton being devoted to Grace Stanley, and Urania being monopolized by the children, it fell out that those four young men, — Orpheus, Frederick, Robert, and Ralph, — were, for a time, thrown together.

Ralph was settled in his new-found realities of life and peace in the Saviour crucified, — the Lord risen indeed. Frederick was bright in a growing experience of *all things in Christ*, — of the presence and sufficiency of that Strong One for all our weakness. Orpheus and Robert loved these truths also, and it was most natural that these four, thrown thus together, spoke out of the abundance of the heart. Ralph, finding that Robert and Orpheus were clear and well-established in their views of the Atonement, felt that he could safely refer to his own past diffi culties on that point, and gave them some ac·count of it, as demonstrating how very evil his heart had been, and how wonderful had been God's forbearance and God's work. Orpheus had never been dissatisfied, he said, as to that doctrine. He had, at one time, been tempted as to the resurrection, not only as to the *doctrine* of the resurrection as accruing to the believer by the resurrection of Christ, but as to Christ *having risen*. All this was passed now. There was not only all the evidence of testimony con-cerning the one, and the word of God for the other; but the *risen* Saviour, — the Lord forever

owning the manhood once assumed,—was henceforth the One worshipped in the sweet, definite
anticipation of being *therein* like Him in His
own time. "Raised in incorruption." This
must be "the redemption of our body," for
which Paul says that we who have the first
fruits of the Spirit do wait.

"It is, no doubt, possible to realize this earnest
waiting, *always*," said Frederick, "but it is only
possible by much prayer, by keeping His words,
by having Him always with us. The manner of
our warfare, the measure of our experience, the
degree of our fellowship with Jesus, depends
very much upon how dear He is to us. But
ultimately all depends upon His gift. "He
giveth more grace." This increase is not to the
proud, but to the humble. And humility, as
God estimates it, seeks subjection to His written
word in all things."

"That is a most sweet work," said Ralph,
"where Saint Peter declares that God 'hath
begotten us again *unto a living hope, by the resurrection of Jesus Christ from the dead.*'"

Orpheus, no longer questioning *the fact*, and the assurances to us therein, yet confessed to some remaining difficulties as to the *significance* of the resurrection of Christ, spiritually considered, and as bearing on Redemption. What was the meaning, for instance, of the expression, "raised again for our justification"? Was there not justification when He once suffered, the Just for the unjust? And then again: "reconciled by His death. . . Saved by His life." Are we not saved by His death?"

"Oh, surely," said Ralph, "but not if He be not risen." *

This *expressed* the truth, but did not *explain* it, and both Ralph and Orpheus looked to Frederick.

"If Jesus' claims were true," said he, "if He was indeed the Son of God, the Saviour, then His resurrection followed of necessity. This was the final, the conclusive proof of all His claims, against which the Jews were so exceed-

* Compare also Romans iv, 25, and v, 9.

ingly mad, and over the announcement of which the Athenians mocked. If He was *not* raised He was not the Lord of life, and need not be received as Messiah indeed. If He *was* risen, then there was nothing to be said by men against His claims, nor any escape from their own guilt. Thus the Apostles at once preached ' Jesus and the resurrection.' The Holy One of God went down into death for a stupendous purpose, but 'it was not possible that He be holden of it.' There is here at once the justification of *His claims* and of *our belief*. Our sins are washed away by His blood. Yet if Christ be not raised, our faith is vain; we are yet in our sins. Not that the atonement is in the resurrection; but, if there is any atonement for sin, there is resurrection, — death being simply the wages of sin." *

" You have said just what I have needed to hear," said Orpheus. " I cannot express to you how glad I am to hear all this, and just as you

* See Supplementary Note, at the end of this volume.

say it. It is *all in the Word of God*, but I needed to have it unfolded. It is a relief to have the difficulties cleared away; indeed, I might say it is a *comfort*," said he, with something more than glad emotion in his tone.

" So it is in the thought of some saint of long ago," said Ralph. " ' *The entrance of Thy words* giveth light.' God always comforts us, I think, by His own word when we are hungry for it. The clear knowledge of the great truth involved in the Lord's resurrection would seem essential to our establishment in faith. Yet it is certain that faith is not knowledge."

" Faith, I think, presupposes a certain amount of knowledge," said Frederick. " How shall they believe on Him of whom they have not heard? *Indoctrination* as to the *foundations* of our faith is the grand *means to* faith. Such knowledge is not faith, but, in God's order, faith waits on it. Then there is spiritual knowledge *beyond* that, without which faith may exist, and always does, in its beginnings. Paul, after hearing of the Colossians' faith in Christ Jesus, and love toward all the saints (that is, toward all the children of God), did not cease to pray for them that they might be *filled with the knowledge of the Lord's will*, in all wisdom and spiritual understanding. It would even seem, from the connection, that we cannot walk (go into daily life) worthy of the Lord, faithful in good works, without this. We need to realize, as to the people of Jesus, how profound our responsibility is to 'add to our faith, *virtue*; and to virtue, *knowledge*.' "

" And more beside," said Orpheus.

" Yes," said Ralph. " He that lacks those things is blind, and cannot see afar off. It is a pity to forget that the call to holiness is *because we have been forgiven*."

" And the end or summing up of all is *love*," said Frederick. " ' And to brotherly kindness, charity.' The end of the commandment is love, but it is qualified as 'out of a pure heart and of a good conscience, and of faith unfeigned.'

Tho rich treasures of instruction in the Epistles, when once the heart is at Jesus' feet, are truly wonderful, and as truly precious. It would be *so good* were we all wholly subject to them!"

"Do you think," asked Orpheus, addressing Ralph, "Do you think that the Christian can live without sin?"

"Oh! don't raise such a question as that," said Ralph, earnestly. "I am just born: and stumbling over the alphabet. What can I know about it? If you mean to ask, can sin ever cease to dwell in the mortal nature; the Scripture says *no*. One's conception of sin must be strangely inadequate if it is imagined to consist solely in what is flagrant and outward. The evil has a deeper root."

"If we know God at all," said Frederick, "we know the things that are freely given to us of Him.* Not as the apostles did, for in knowledge, as in all else, there is first, beginning, then, increase. But, in Him, we go from

*1st Cor. ii : 12.

strength to strength.. We know what is the fruit of the Spirit, and we soon learn what is the warfare against the flesh. Let us allow the fruit to grow, and let us war a good warfare."

"We hear so much," said Orpheus, "about *out of the seventh of Romans, into the eighth,* and more of the same sort."

"Well," said Ralph, rather wearily, "as I said, don't ask me about it. I know that walking in the light, as He is in the light, will keep us in the confession of sin. The seventh of Romans I should think is, in its general tenor, bondage, or temptation ; in which case the eighth is adoption and peace."

"That is good," said Frederick. "We who love the Saviour hold fast His commandments, and seek to *do* them ; but not that we may inflate ourselves with the idea of sinless attainment."

"No," said Ralph, "not that we may get what He has already given us."

* * * * * * * *

At this moment Janie came at somebody's bidding to protest that Ralph was keeping his three friends from all the Stanleys, and was not himself at all attentive to the company. She slipped her hand as usual into Ralph's, who greeted her with his usual low-spoken "Janie, little Janie." They moved toward the company in the other parlor, who, as it proved were waiting for some of Orpheus' music. Robert took the guitar for a soliloquy on the verandah, but Mrs. Stanley would allow nothing of the kind, and, at her request, he sat at the piano while Orpheus took the flute. And the music spoke only of gladness, and peace, and thanksgiving. Following this were a few songs; refined in thought, and fine in melody; after Orpheus' own taste, which could select no other.

Then when, after some time, Mr. and Mrs. Clayton, with Miss Penelope, came in, the pastime was laid aside, and the company fell again into groups, and the conversation flowed on.

22

So the afternoon passed away, and evening shadows gathered ; and tea was set out in the library. And, when Mr. Clayton had referred the giving of thanks to Frederick, the conversation fell, without constraint or forethought, into channels that led the thoughts upward, and the day closed luminous with truth more sweetly realized, and the bright unseen more near. Luminous, that is, to all except three who were less happy than the others.   For Herbert Clayton did not see that it was worth while to bore one another with such sentiments, and his affianced Grace did not pretend to any interest in them ; while Mr. Clayton, who was quite at home on any subject when occasion arose, sailed good-naturedly on the current because the tide set that way.

.   .   .   .

Late at night Ralph was alone, reading from the Psalms. And a glad thought from that Hymnal of God fell through his soul like a lullaby and mingled with all his dreams : --

IN THY PRESENCE IS FULNESS OF JOY; AT THY RIGHT HAND ARE PLEASURES FOREVER-MORE.

CHAPTER XVI.

RETURN HOME.

T was found advisable for Mrs. Cushing not to prolong her stay into the Tennessee winter, beyond the middle of December. And so it came to pass that the holidays found them delightfully settled with their "other cousins," as Ralph called the Farr family, in their pleasant home near Baton Rouge. The plan was to remain, if God pleased, until the first of April: and, returning northward, to delay during April at the Stanleys' again; by which means they would escape the vicissitudes of that unsettled month at the North. And so Ralph reluctantly withdrew from the law-office, and from all the scenes so recently entered and already so endeared.

And yet, (so many sided are we) there was no lack of enthusiasm about a sail down the Mississippi, and a winter green with bay and cypress trees, and ruddy with roses and oleanders and all the soft light of a misplaced springtime. As to regrets at personal partings, there were a few that Ralph confessed uppermost. In these regrets Frederick, and Orpheus, and Janie largely shared. But Zedekiah was wholly glad to be sent home by steamboat and freight-cars, with Penn and Philip and the carriage. The fellow had seen enough of the world and of nothing to do. He reported to William and Margaret that Mr. Ralph was " wonderfully changed, and had a word now and then about the Lord Jesus that fell out of his lips too softly for one to resist." Margaret wept for gladness; but Zed only looked puzzled, and said it must be a fine thing to be a Christiar

In March, however, all idea of delaying at the Stanleys' through April was abandoned, owing to trouble at home, — the severe illness of Mr. Cushing, and Rebekah's overwhelming cares. We must turn for a little while to the scenes there, and note down in brief the history of the month of March as it transpired with Rebekah.

Mr. Cushing had softened wonderfully in his general tone and mien during the six months of real trial that the great change in his home involved. He was, as we have seen before, a man of strong will and plenty of pride; and, his determination once made that his wife should have all the benefit possible from the complete carrying out of the change as first planned; his pride alone, if nothing higher, would not allow him to swerve or to retract. But there was a higher principle at work with Mr. Cushing in this instance. There were many silent hours, both before and following the departure, when he had been led to reveiw the past with sufficient candor to perceive that selfishness had been dominant in his nature, to the impoverishing of his own life and the embittering of others. He saw virtues in his wife and children that he coveted and knew he did not possess. The gentleness, the generosity, the carefulness for others welfare, and the charity for others faults, — those traits that so fully adorned the mother's life, and, under her training, were enlarging in the children, he became aware had been bearing with strong, silent energy upon him these many years, and had rendered his life richer than it could have been without their contact; yet had been strangely unnoticed, unfelt, unfollowed. In his absorbed selfishness he had thought himself acute, sensitive, suffering greatly from slight causes. Now he began to discern that he had been obtuse, insensible, and causing rather than enduring a suffering worthy the name. Indeed, *endurance*, in the correct sense, being a high moral quality, there could be no endurance in fostering his own woe at the crossing of his own whims. And there could certainly be nothing lovely or excellent in blessing himself on account of his own ease and acquisitions. All this had been opening up to him. There was a something in the combined anxiety of Ralph and Rebekah for their mother which jarred upon his own dormant affections, and rang out a contrast so clear that the flash of sound awoke prolonged reverberations which he must needs ponder. And, as himself grew less, wife, and son, and daughter, and all mankind enlarged in his regard. Thus it was that, as the months rolled on, the absent wife and the present daughter were both more correctly appreciated than ever before; not only because justice to them had never been possible in the temper of his past, but equally because the one made herself estimated by stepping out of the place she had filled, and the other by the large humility and patience of her filial endeavor as far as possible to fill the vacant place. Thus it was, also, that the simple satisfaction with which he had at first met Ralph's assent to his own will in the matter of professional aim, gave place to genuine appreciation of the sacrifice, and to some dawning sympathy for the youth whose tastes might be the index of what his life should be. His manful endeavor to do what he hated was (Mr. Cushing still preferred to think) greater proof of his ability to do it than any possible success; while it argued likewise (he began to believe) some fine filial principle at bottom. On the whole he felt for Ralph, and estimated him more kindly, if not more fairly, than of old. He could not in any degree share Rebekah's joy at Ralph's confession of Christ, because not himself in a position or a state that would enable him to have any part with them in that joy. But, in the better and less bitter mood that now prevailed with him, he thought it might be a very good thing, and would not wish to put anything in his way. If he made as real a Christian as his mother, he would, Mr. Cushing thought, make none the worse lawyer.

From the first of March to the first of May !

Only two months! In looking back over the five and a half months of autumn dreariness and winter snows already past since the absent ones left, the two months of opening spring that should now intervene before their return seemed little, and might be quickly over. So thought Rebekah, who was already five years older in experience, and stronger beyond compute, for the school of responsibility, and of all gentle virtues, in which she had been so nobly exercised while making light, and peace, and patient rule in her father's house. [The gentle virtues, dear reader, are hard of attainment, and are a possession of strength when attained. If any doubt it, let them put to proof this that is said, with God's word shining on their lives.]

It was just as March entered. Windily, keenly, roughly, bitterly cold. In short, Marchly. Albeit they say this may be either " like a lion " or " like a lamb." Such is March. And with his leonic aspect entire and undisguised he greeted Apple Downs this year. Rebekah was sitting in the library, where by reason of her father's growing sociability, she passed most of her time. It was now toward evening, and warm in that cheerful room. In fact, it was always warm there. William never allowed the furnace fire to flag. The warmly-built house luxuriated in open registers at every corner ; and, that things might *look* warm also, there was always a fire of glowing coals in the library grate. It was natural, therefore, that Rebekah should be warm. She had been over and over the house to-day without a sensation of cold. She had done all the mending in her mamma's sitting-room, and all the overseeing demanded by Jane and Joan and Margaret, and all the letter-writing, and reading, and fine sewing in the library, in quiet oblivion to the outside weather. She had even stepped over to the snug abode of William and Margaret, a few rods in the rear, to see to their comfort, and encourage little Willie who was getting well of a cold, — a " reel hard one " Margaret declared it had been. But there was sunshine all the way, and the house broke the force of the wind, and there was sunshine in her own heart and in the cottage she entered. So that Rebekah had really forgotten that it was a *very* cold, a *very* disagreeable day. But now, as she sat in the library, and the sun, who was making longer visits than his shortest, looked brightly, coldly over a black cloud when he was going down, and the wind howled through the maples, and slapped the little willow twigs against the windows, Rebekah, still warm, shivered in sympathy with what she saw and heard out of doors, and in sympathy with what she thought of. For her father had gone in the sleigh with Zedekiah a two-mile drive to see to the family of Edward Winn, who were suffering from sickness, and, she feared also, from the cold. There were not many families in the county to whom it was possible to offer " charitable assistance " at any season of the year; and cases of indigence were rare about Apple Downs. But Edward Winn being not " steady' ' and his wife feeble, and the children sick, there seemed ample occasion for "seeing to" them — for the wife's and children's sake, if not for Edward's. At breakfast that morning Rebekah had mentioned to her father that she had not been to them nor heard from them for a week, and that a severe sore throat would disappoint her of going to-day. At this intelligence Mr. Cushing had declared his willingness to go in her place; for, as has been mentioned, his regard for the good estate of his fellow-mortals had been on the increase of late. This was one of its first manifestations in a practical way, on which account Rebekah had been doubly glad to accept the proposition.

Mr. Cushing had not started on his unwonted errand until afternoon, being previously occupied with some business papers, and naturally a little slow to move in the new direction. But it was now past the time for him to return, and "What could keep papa so long?" was a question that Rebekah was uneasily asking herself. She feared

all was not as well at the Winns'.   And then she
thought of the children's sewing-circle, which
should meet to-morrow, and how happy the little
faces would be when she announced the receipt
of their box of clothing by the missionary's family a long way off, and the great service it had
been to them.   And that her mamma (the dear,
missed, longed-for mother) was not at home
yet, was really a matter of gratulation with Rebekah, in view of the severe times in their
latitude.   Ralph was having a fine time in Louisiana, and Baton Rouge was as good for law-
studies as Mariondale.   He found there no one
to exactly fill the place of the Claytons and the
Jamesons; neither were the Farrs by any means
the Stanleys.   (There were no children, and
especially no Janie.)   But Mr. Pleadgood was,
on the whole, as agreeable as Judge Hazelton,
and had a library equally fine.   Mrs. Cushing
continued to make good advance in strength,
and in every physical good hoped for.   These
were the general contents of their recent letters,

which sometimes overflowed, also, with Ralph's growing experience of truth through a growing acquaintance with the Saviour, and, thus, with himself, the saved and still needy one. But, for all this, Ralph's letters said very little about himself, for the reason that the Holy Spirit leads us to speak not of self but of Christ; and, if of His work in us, yet in a way to keep not *self* in view, but Jesus the Lord. Mrs. Cushing's letters were often laden with the mother's joy in her son's establishment in grace, and in his growing subjection to the Word of God; as also in all his natural expansion and settledness of character. His companionship, both toward herself and their friends, she said, was really a ministration. Her letters, too, were marked by glad longing to return, and by tender appreciation of the two at home, and tender thankfulness toward God. There was every promise of confirmed health in her own case, and of good ability to stay at home when once happily there again.

The sun had quite set when the sleigh drove around the house, and Mr. Cushing came in. If there had been less to say about the Winns, and less light in his eye from the consciousness of having ministered comfort and relief where these were needed, Rebekah might have noticed that he looked strangely tired for him, and that his animation was of pleasant excitement, not of his normal power. As it was, this passed just then unnoticed. The poor family was badly off indeed, — their fuel all gone, their provisions low, and one of the children worse. Edward realized the situation sadly, and with expressions of penitence, but lacked energy to look for work. And, indeed, all available hands were needed at home. The flannel and the blankets, and the provisions, that Rebekah had sent, had brought tears of joy. Mr. Cushing, seeing the sickness and the grief, and that Edward was trying to help his wife, had no heart to reproach him for not being at work; but had suggested that, if he had wood at hand,

he would be well occupied in cutting and split-
ting it, and keeping two rooms well warmed.
He had, therefore, driven on half a mile to
Farmer Closefist's, and paid him for a cord of
maple wood and a half-cord of mixed hemlock
and chestnut, on condition that he would haul it
at once to the Winns. Mr. Closefist was a bach-
elor. His niece, Ann Freeman, who, with her
sister Ruth, kept his house in order, did not
know that they were so "bad off" at Edward's,
and did feel sorry for his wife and those poor
children, but thought Edward was "a hard
case," — worth saving if he could be saved; but
could he be saved? Hadn't Mr. Hidden "tried
and tried" to reform him, and "labored" to
convert him? Hadn't Elder Jones given him
work, and given him counsel, and shown him
kindness, long after most folks had given him
up? Ann was afraid there was no use in
hoping anything for Edward. But Ruth would
ride over on the load of maple, and see if she
might stay to-night, and so allow Mrs. Winn to

23

sleep without care. That was the best of all, Rebekah thought, and clapped her hands for Ruth. How happy that her father had gone on to Closefist's instead of looking for wood at Farmer Black's on the way home. Mr. Black was a good man, and would have sent the wood more heartily, but he had no Ruth who could watch with the children and take the mother's care. Certainly God was caring for that sorrowful mother and those little ones; and who could say but He was cherishing thoughts of mercy toward Edward also?

Mr. Cushing had remained a good while at the Winns, and had delayed also at Closefist's, — in the first place, to push the man up to the work and see that he was actually loading the sled with wood; and, secondly, for the surprised pleasure he found in the simple, decorous manners and conversation of Ruth Freeman and her sister Ann. Ruth, he said, had excused herself for not sitting down. She was stepping about all the time that he was in their nice kitchen, doing various work; the main items of which were, as far as he could see, the getting herself and a pumpkin pie ready to ride to the Winns' on the maple wood. In all this Rebekah was of course profoundly interested, as was Mr. Cushing also. And it was only when Joan rang the bell for tea that he was himself aware of being chilly, and returned to consciousness of certain vague pains that had been traversing his bones on the drive homeward. As the narrative was finished, and his animation faded off, Rebekah noticed how exceedingly tired he looked. But he thought the fatigue and ill feeling would pass off with the refreshment of tea-drinking. And the tea did refresh, but he found that he could eat nothing; and the chilliness became more marked during the evening, and the weariness more painful; so that, for an unheard-of thing, he inclined to retire early. And then the impression that this was only the beginning of a sickness that might require nursing, settled down upon him with the weight of conviction.

He thought himself foolish, but he could not shake off the despondency. And, though not increasing Rebekah's apprehensions by expressing his own conviction, it led him to say to her (in that considerateness which had marked him of late) that he had often had the thought — if either of them should be sick her mother ought not to be sent for peremptorily, nor even alarmed. "It ought not to be," he said. "The distance is so great, that a sickness, once severe, would probably find its issue one way or another before she could reach home. And a sudden return before the weather is suitable, and under all the fatigue of rapid travel, might, and probably would, work sore ill to her."

The next day Mr. Cushing was unrefreshed, and every way worse. In the afternoon Doctor Saywell called and pronounced the case pneumonia. It was impossible to say, so early, whether it would be of light or severe type. Mr. Cushing's general vigor was good, and the disease was one usually well recovered from at his time of life, if uncomplicated by other disease.

Poor Rebekah! whether the type should be light or severe, this was a heavy trial to her. But she should be sustained. She knew the promise could not fail. She believed her father would not die. She would not alarm her mother. She would bear it alone for her mother's sake. But how *could* she bear it alone? Then she remembered and knew that she was *not* alone; and in the thanksgiving that arose out of this thought she was comforted.

But Rebekah had never seen sickness like this. It grew worse from day to day. The weakness became extreme. Even the mind lost all its independence, and at last all its clearness and power. A great deal of the nursing had to be left to William; for, happily, William was a clever nurse. Doctor Saywell was, humanly, everything. Rebekah hung upon his words. She knew he would tell her the truth. He candidly encouraged, and found no cause for great anxiety until the eighth day, when the opposite lung became slightly invaded, and delirium set in. The case was grave; but the general symptoms, under the circumstances, were good. There was no positive sinking.

"What shall I write mamma now? or shall I telegraph?" asked Rebekah.

"What have you written previously?" asked the doctor in response.

"Every day a few words, saying that papa was doing well for one so sick, and that he did not wish her to move.

"I would not telegraph. If your mother were strong, or if she were within two days ride, it would be the best way. But, as it is, the telegram would alarm too much; the strain would be too great; and her arrival here five or six days from now might be to find your father better and herself much worse. Write her the truth: that Mr. Cushing is in some respects not as well; that the case is, in fact, more grave; but that the general symptoms do not discourage; that we think she had better not move in haste; and to hope for brighter news in another letter."

"And do you think — do you think?" faltered Rebekah.

"My dear Miss Cushing," said the doctor, "I think nothing; I hope everything. Pneumonia, affecting both lungs, is always very serious. But in this case the lung last affected is but slightly so as yet. Your father's constitution is remarkably vigorous, and his strength is still such as to encourage hope. We are warranted in hoping everything to-day. Let us not burden ourselves with to-morrow."

. . . .

And Mr. Clearwater came arm in arm with dear old Doctor Laidley. No professional jealousy there; no anti-Christian offishness, nor etiquette, subversive of love and the labor thereof. Doctor Laidley might have called alone for that matter, which he very well knew; for he knew Frank Clearwater through and through. But the young minister had called at the house on his way to the Cushings; in the spirit of Christ, taking his old brother's arm and walking him off (not by constraint, but finding his feet willing as ever) to join with him in sympathy and in prayer. And, as those two loving, sorrowful faces greeted Rebekah and entered the sick-room, they seemed to her like the faces of angels.

 . . . .

A few days later Rebekah thought her father must be a little better, and looked inquiringly at Doctor Saywell. His look and manner assured her that she was not wrong. How her heart bounded! How her weary eyes lightened, and her aching temples were forgotten!

"What shall I write mother to-day?" she asked.

"Write her," said Doctor Saywell, "that if she will be here the first week in April she will, we think, find the sick man fully convalescent. As his convalescence is the stage during which your mother can be of real service, without too great strain upon herself, she need have no regrets or scruples about having been away during the sickness, and it would be unfair, both to you and to your father, to urge her staying away longer. Advise her to come by steamboat to Cincinnati; or, if possible, to Wheeling or Pittsburg, so reducing the travel by rail to the minimum."

·   ·   ·   ·   ·   ·   ·   ·

Oh! there was new light in the house that day! Long before evening the letter was written, by which Mrs. Cushing and Ralph would be made to rejoice with Rebekah, and would be upheld in their decision already made, on no account to delay after the month of March was fairly passed. Rebekah slept that night as not for near three weeks before. And, the day following, Mr. Cushing was himself sensible of being better, and was glad of the good word sent the absent ones; only still a little solicitous lest Mrs. Cushing were coming North too early.

But Rebekah reminded him that there could be no severe cold in April to keep her within doors, which was the chief source of evil to her. And, after that, the anticipation of her speedy return sustained him, and quickened his recovery.

Sitting one day, or half reclining, in dressing-gown and easy-chair, a few days before the anticipated arrival, he suddenly asked Rebekah, " Do you think Ralph still has longings toward a chair in literature or language, as at first ? "

" Oh, I dare say, yes," said Rebekah. " You have seen all his letters, except those received while you have been sick; and you know he has only once or twice made the barest allusion to it. More than ever, since he became a Christian, he seems cheerfully bent upon the law. But then you know it never can be to his taste, nor quite fill out his life."

Mr. Cushing sighed, and Rebekah thought him tired, and that he had been sitting long enough. But he disclaimed being tired, and said that he must talk a few minutes.

"I cannot bear to think," he said, " of Ralph drying away in a professor's chair. He is of too large a soul, and of too lively gifts, for disquisitional addresses, and stated recitations, and all the stiff enclosure of a professor's destiny. Opportunity to act on the minds and lives of men in his own free, large, living way, is what he needs for full development. And the legal profession is not a poor field for that. But there is a better one."

" The medical ? " asked Rebekah, distrustfully ; for she did not believe it would be better for Ralph.

Nor did Mr. Cushing. " Medicine," he said, " might be placed before law in some respects. But Ralph's tastes would certainly be more averse to it on the whole. And, now that his mind is settled as to the Christian faith and doctrine, I am thinking that the ministry would afford him as good scope as the law."

" Papa ! Why, papa ! how singular you are !" exclaimed Rebekah, fairly bursting into tears.

She did not know why. And, drawing her chair closer to her father's, she put her head on his shoulder and wept there, — for the first time in her life since babyhood.

"Indeed I *must* be singular to make you weep just now," said her father; "I thought I should make you glad."

"Oh! you do, you do," she sobbed, "but give me time to speak."

And then, when her commotion of relief, and surprise, and joy had a little subsided, she went over the subject calmly, gravely, — thinking it too serious, and involving issues too immense, to be weighed in the scale of natural talent only, or considered in a vein of mere taste.

"Yes, I suppose so," answered her father. "And I would hold Ralph back from his old scheme more kindly than I used to, but not less firmly. I think it should be the law or the ministry with him. I will not dictate between the two."

"But it is something quite new and strange

with you, papa, to think favorably of the ministry for *any one*, is it not?"

"It must seem so to you," he said. Then, pausing, he added, "I have no doubt it is really the very highest calling a man can enter, and the hardest to adorn. So there is at once a plea for and against it. This conviction is somewhat new with me. But, for myself, I am, I fear, just where I have been always."

But his words indicated to Rebekah that he was not just where, or as, he had been. It seemed to her good that her father was *beginning to fear.*

CHAPTER XVII.

CONCLUSION.

IFTEEN years have passed away. The light and shade of those years have been various to Ralph, and to all Ralph's own. What remains to be said on these few pages touches Ralph chiefly; and it touches his present more than the rich, happy, toilsome part embraced in the years intervening between the scenes we have recorded, and the scenes of to-day.

A petition that stands in living utterance

among the pages of Thomas à Kempis, crossed Ralph's eye, and fell sweetly, wondrously, through his heart, one day when his whole soul was one living petition that God would lead him into works of obedience, not of self-pleasing; and that He would keep him out of the Gospel ministry unless He were Himself leading him into it. And that prayer, answered then, lives in his heart still; and, in one language or another, is uttered every day: "Remember Thy tender mercies and fill my heart with Thy grace, Thou who wilt not have Thy works to be empty."

Sometimes this supplication finds utterance in the language of Scripture itself; as, "Uphold me according unto Thy word, that I may live; and let me not be ashamed of my hope." Or again: "In the way of Thy judgments, O Lord, have we waited for Thee. The desire of our soul is to Thy name, and to the remembrance of Thee." And sometimes the language is drawn from no source but that of the heart's fellowship with the Lord through the indwelling Spirit: and has no record but on high where Jesus is.

And this living frame of dependence, and of the expression of it, is that which has kept Ralph Cushing lowly, and strong in the Lord only, during near twelve years of increasing influence, and of blessed success, in preaching the Gospel and expounding the truth as it is in Jesus.

From the hearty, jovial, thoughtful youth he has, through many temptations and much warfare, passed on into the still hearty, still jovial, but earnest, serious man. He early found, through the learning of lessons, sorrowful but salutary to himself, that he could do nothing without the fellowship (the indwelling and the converse) of Christ the Lord. And he is still learning in the school in which God has placed him both to learn and to teach; having, in his own case, made a little of the sweet experience: " I can do all things through Christ, who strengthens me." The sweetest, dearest word in all the universe to him is *Saviour.* And although the words of the epistle, " Unto you, therefore, who believe, He is precious," have more than once been the theme of his discourse, he has never yet finished expounding them.

Ralph still looks back with strong emotion and amazement upon the events of the winter in the South, as the turning-point in his life, and, to all human appearance, the seal of his destiny. He has long had the love and esteem of a large community, and of a devoted church, all of which is reciprocated in the bonds of manhood, and in the bonds of Christ. But there is something peculiar in the affection with which he often turns toward the scenes and the persons of those brightest spots on earth, — his father's house and the three houses around Mariondale. He still loves and cherishes his mother as he cherished and loved her then; or yet the more tenderly because of sorrow that has followed. As long ago as Ralph became the settled minister, Rebekah esteemed herself the settled old maid; married to filial duty; and too satisfied, she said, with parental love and the service granted her at home to look for, wish for, or accept of any other. And "Rebekah" is a name that Ralph speaks often; always softly, sometimes out of tears.

But Ralph has a home, a sweet home of his own; a home for which he waited long, in quiet assurance that it would be made at last. Ten years after the child Janie first ministered to him he met her again, in her fair maidenhood of seventeen. And then he told her what he had been waiting all these years to tell: that he loved none so well as her, nor could any other be his wife. Three years ago they were united in bonds that only death can sunder. And now, often, in that happy home where the Saviour reigns, and the peace of God is shed abroad, are heard lowly, softly, gladly, the words so often uttered in the same tones long ago, "Janie, little Janie!"

SUPPLEMENTARY NOTE.

(Page 279.)

FOR the sake of those who are shaken, as Orpheus was not, concerning *the reality* of the Lord's resurrection, the following striking extract is given from a recent author, — *Edmond de Pressense*, of the French Evangelical Church.

" We know that [the resurrection of Christ] is one of the miracles at which unbelief most of all stumbles, and which appears to it altogether absurd and impossible. It argues skilfully upon the laws of our physical being; it demonstrates with force and clearness that, from a natural point of view, the principle of life, once extinct, cannot be revived; and it treats the resurrection of our Saviour as a ridiculous fable. As for ourself, between a physical impossibility and a moral impossibility we do not hesitate. The second seems to us alone absolute and invincible. We also believe the permanence and the inflexibility of the law of creation. But that law which is the axis around which all things turn is not a material law; it is a moral law. The laws of the physical world are of necessity subordinate to it. It is because of this that God has already shaken the earth;* and it is in order to give to it a supreme consecration that He has said, *I will shake yet once more not only the earth, but also the heavens*; as if to show us, in a manner the most solemn, that the whole of the natural laws which rule the exterior world is nothing in His eyes compared to the fundamental law of the Scriptural world. Let them not speak

*Heb. xii : 26, 27.

to us, then, of the impossibility of the resurrection. That which is impossible an Apostle proceeds to tell us: *It was not possible*, says Saint Peter, *that He should be held in the bands of death.** That could not be, because death, being the wages of sin, the justice of God would be at fault if Jesus Christ were held in its bands after the redemption sacrifice. God would not know how to demand again the payment of a debt already cancelled [the judgment of a people fully acquitted]. These bands of death ought, then, to break for Jesus Christ, in the name of a necessity higher than all the necessities of the natural order. It is impossible that He be held there, as it is impossible that God be unjust."†

And we may add that, God (with whom all moral principles are as immutable as God is) has declared that while " things that are made " shall be " shaken " and " removed," there are " things which cannot be shaken," and which shall remain.

* Acts, ii ; 24.

† Le Redemption ; (Paris 1858. See Page 297).

MARGARET SIDNEY'S BOOKS.

That "Child Classic," **FIVE LITTLE PEPPERS AND HOW THEY GREW**, comes out in a new, charming edition. $1.50

The perfect reproduction of child life in its minutest phases catches one's attention at once. — *Christian Advocate.*

SO AS BY FIRE. $1.25.

We have followed with intense interest the story of David Folsom. — *Woman at Work.*

THE PETTIBONE NAME. $1.25.

This is a capital story illustrating New England life. — *Inter-Ocean*, Chicago.

The characters of the story seem to be studies from life. — *Boston Post.*

HALF YEAR AT BRONCKTON. $1.25.

A lively boy writes, "This is about the best book that ever was written or ever can be."

HOW THEY WENT TO EUROPE. 16mo, illustrated.

The plan of the book resembles, in some respects, that of "A Voyage Around my Room." It is certainly bright. — *N. Y. Independent.*

THE GOLDEN WEST. Extra cloth, $2.25; boards, $1.75.

The best travel book for children. It combines fun with instruction in the right proportions. The pictures of the States west of the Mississippi and along the sunny Pacific slopes, are full of graphic coloring.

WHO TOLD IT TO ME? $1.25.

A most stirring story of school life in New England. The characters make their mark in the war for the Union. It is such a book as you would expect from Margaret Sidney.

WHAT THE SEVEN DID. Boards, $1.75; extra cloth, $2.25.

A royal gift book for children. They read it again and again, and, best of all, they practice it. Many Wordsworth Clubs are doing deeds of charity according to the model in this book.

A NEW DEPARTURE FOR GIRLS. 75 cents.

The most practical, sensible and to-the-point book which has been written for girls within the last fifty years — a godsend to the "Helen Harknesses" of our great cities, and small towns as well. That this kindly effort has already reached young women is evident from advertisements already appearing in the "Wanted" columns of the Boston dailies.

POLLY: Where she lived, what she said and what she Did. Quarto, 50 cents.

With twelve full-page pictures by Margaret Johnson. A story of a funny parrot and two charming children.

ON EASTER DAY. An illustrated poem. 35 cents.

THE MINUTE MAN. A ballad of the "shot heard round the world." Illustrated, $1.50.

HESTER, and other New England Stories. A story for adults. $1.25.

The character touches are strong and well-defined. It is fresh with New England atmosphere.

TWO MODERN LITTLE PRINCES, and other Stories for young people. $1.00.

Full of exquisite touches of humor and pathos, and cosey home life.

BOOKS FOR BOYS.

ALL AMONG THE LIGHTHOUSES. By MARY BRADFORD CROWNINSHIELD, wife of Commander Crowninshield. Finely illustrated from photographs and original drawings. Extra cloth, quarto, $2.50.

An attractive book for boys, giving the account of an actual trip along the coast of Maine by a lighthouse inspector with two wide awake boys in charge. The visits to the numerous lighthouses not only teem with incident, but abound in information that will interest every one.

BOYS' HEROES. By EDWARD EVERETT HALE. Reading Union Library. 16mo, illustrated, cloth, $1.00.

Twelve chapters containing the story told in Dr. Hale's characteristic style, of a dozen characters famed in history as worthy to bear the title of heroes, and the story of whose deeds and lives possesses a special interest for boys.

PLUCKY BOYS. Business Boys' Library. By the author of "John Halifax, Gentleman," and other authors. $1.00.

"A pound of pluck is worth a ton of luck."— *President Garfield.* Spirited narratives of boys who have conquered obstacles and become successful business men ; or of other young fellows who have shown fearlessness and "fight" in situations of danger.

A BOY'S WORKSHOP. By A BOY AND HIS FRIENDS. $1.00.

Just the book for boys taking their first lesson in the use of tools. All sorts of practical suggestions and sound advice, with valuable illustrations fill the volume.

BOY LIFE IN THE UNITED STATES NAVY. By H. H. CLARK. 12mo, illustrated, $1.50.

If there is anything in the way of human attire which more than any other commands the admiration and stirs the enthusiasm of the average boy of whatever nation, it is the trim uniform and shining buttons that distinguish the jolly lads of the "Navy." In this graphically written and wonderfully entertaining volume, boy life in the Navy of the United States is described by a naval officer, in a manner which cannot fail to satisfy the boys.

HOW SUCCESS IS WON. By MRS. SARAH K. BOLTON. $1.00.

This is the best of the recent books of this popular class of biography ; all its "successful men" are Americans, and with two or three exceptions they are living and in the full tide of business and power. In each case, the facts have been furnished to the author by the subject of the biography, or by family friends ; and Mrs. Bolton has chosen from this authentic material those incidents which most fully illustrate the successive steps and the ruling principles, by which success has been gained. A portrait accompanies each biography.

STORIES OF DANGER AND ADVENTURE. By ROSE G. KINGSLEY, B. P. SHILLABER, FREDERIC SCHWATKA and others. $1.25.

Fascinating stories of thrilling incidents in all sorts of places and with all kinds of people. Very fully illustrated.

WONDER STORIES OF TRAVEL. By ELIOT McCORMICK, ERNEST INGERSOLL, E. E. BROWN, DAVID KER and others. Fully illustrated. $1.50.

From the opening story, "A Boy's Race with General Grant at Ephesus," to the last, "A Child in Florence," this book is full of stir and interest. Indian, Italian, Chinese, German, English, Scotch, French, Arabian and Egyptian scenes and people are described, and there is such a feast of good things one hardly knows which to choose first.

BOOKS FOR GIRLS.

HOLD UP YOUR HEADS, GIRLS! By Annie H. Ryder. $1.00.

One of the brightest, breeziest books for girls ever written; as sweet and wholesome as the breath of clover on a clear June morning, and as full of life and inspiration as a trumpet call. The writer, a popular teacher, speaks of what she knows, and has put her own magnetism into these little plain, sensible, earnest talks, and the girls will read them and be thrilled by them as by a personal presence.

A NEW DEPARTURE FOR GIRLS. By Margaret Sidney. 75 cents.

In this bright little story, we see what may be really done in the way of self-support by young women of sturdy independence and courage, with no false pride to deter them from taking up the homely work which they are capable of doing. It will give an incentive to many a baffled, discouraged girl who has failed from trying to work in the old ruts.

HOW THEY LEARNED HOUSEWORK. By Christina Goodwin. 75 cents.

Four merry schoolgirls during vacation time are inducted into the mysteries of chamber-work, cooking, washing, ironing, putting up preserves and cutting and making underclothes, all under the careful supervision of one of the mothers. The whole thing is made attractive for them in a way that is simply captivating, and the story of their experiment is full of interest.

A GIRL'S ROOM. With plans and designs for work upstairs and down, and entertainments for herself and friends. By Some Friends of the Girls. $1.00.

This dainty volume not only shows girls how to make their rooms cosey and attractive at small trouble and expense, but also how to pass a social evening with various games, and to prepare many pretty and useful articles for themselves and friends.

CHRISTIE'S CHRISTMAS. By Pansy. 12mo, fully illustrated $1.50.

Christie is one of those delightfully life-like, naïve and interesting characters which no one so well as Pansy can portray, and in the study of which every reader will find delight and profit.

ANNA MARIA'S HOUSEKEEPING. By Mrs. S. D. Power 16mo, extra cloth, $1.00.

Articles on household matters, written in a clear, fascinating style out of the experience of a writer who knows whereof she speaks. Every girl and young housekeeper should own a copy.

BRAVE GIRLS. By Mary Hartwell Catherwood, Nora Perry, Mrs. John Sherwood and others. $1.50.

Here are deeds of stirring adventure and peril, and quiet heroism no less brave, to incite girls to be faithful and fearless, strong and true to the right.

NEW EVERY MORNING: Selections of Readings for Girls. By Annie H. Ryder. $1.00.

This is just such a book as one would expect from the popular author of "Hold up your Heads, Girls!" and will be no less a favorite. The selections are all choice and appropriate, and will be eagerly read each morning by the happy owners.

THE POT OF GOLD.

BY MARY E. WILKINS.

12mo, $1.50. Fully Illustrated.

A new book by Miss Wilkins is an event in literature, and an announcement of the first volume of her juvenile stories will be welcomed not only by young people but by all who have come to love and honor her for her wonderfully faithful pictures of New England life.

The realistic element which is so marked a feature of her stories for adults is blended with another style of writing in the collection which makes up "The Pot of Gold." Heretofore we have seen Miss Wilkins at her best in her simple, natural portraitures of plain, homely country folk, whose humble joys and sorrows she has painted with wonderful skill. But there is another side to her nature, in which she fairly revels in the fanciful, the humorous and the romantic, and delights in giving the reins to her imagination. Nothing can be more delicious than these flights of fancy and the fun and drollery with which they abound.

The last part of the volume is made up of stories of child life in the olden days of New England, and describes some of the customs of those earlier times, when childhood was not the paradise it now is. These have the flavor of the soil, and are as quaint and old-fashioned as the characters themselves. Many an older reader will delight in these quaint, old-time pictures of Puritan days.

The book is beautifully gotten up, printed on superfine paper, with illustrations by W. L. Taylor, Childe Hassam, Barnes, Bridgman and other popular artists The binding, in robin's-egg blue with gold and silver design, is simply exquisite.

₊ *At the bookstores, or sent postpaid on receipt of price, by*

EXQUISITE GIFT BOOKS.

The Poet's Year.

Edited by OSCAR FAY ADAMS. Oblong 4to, super-calendered paper. 150 illustrations, of which 25 are full-page drawings by Chaloner. Gold cloth, $6.00; morocco, $10.00.

"The Poet's Year" is the happy execution of an admirable and original idea.

It is a volume of carefully selected poetry of the seasons, and embraces not only the choicest gems of the older poets, but an almost endless variety of selections from famous and popular writers of the day, with numerous original poems contributed especially for the purpose.

It would be difficult to find a more delightful and diversified collection of poems illustrative of the beauties of nature and the manifold human emotions inspired by them. The whole make-up of the book is in keeping with its contents, forming one of the most beautiful gift-books of the year.

Out of Doors with Tennyson.

Edited, with Introduction, by ELBRIDGE S. BROOKS. Fully illustrated with views of the localities of the poems. Quarto, $2.50.

Such poems and portions of poems written by the Laureate as have to do with out-door life in any way — "The Brook," of course, and the "Garden Song" in Maud, and many others. One is hardly aware of the many exquisite descriptions of pastoral scenes in Tennyson's poetry until he finds them gathered in this delightful volume which will have a special charm for all lovers of the beautiful in nature, as well as all admirers of the poet.

"What endears Tennyson to me is his handling of the everyday sights and sounds of nature. He has learnt to see that in all in nature, in the hedge-row and sand bank as well as the Alp peak and th ocean waste, is a true sublimily, and ever-fertile garden of poetic images."
CHARLES KINGSLEY.

The True Story of
Christopher Columbus

Called the Admiral

Told for Youngest Readers by ELBRIDGE S. BROOKS, author of " Historic Boys," " The Story of the American Sailor," " The Story of the United States," etc.

Bound in elegant illuminated cover, with coat of arms of Spain and the United States, together with elaborate decorations,

PRICE, $1.25 ; EXTRA CLOTH, $1.50

It is with the desire to picture for younger readers the real Columbus, that Mr. Brooks has prepared for the children his " True Story of Christopher Columbus." There is so much of interest, so much that is stirring, striking, absorbing and dramatic in the real story of the adventures, the trials and the success of the great Italian who found a New World. that it does not need the time-worn fables or the hectic over-statements of an earlier day to emphasize the story or halo the life of the great Admiral.

The book is profusely illustrated, is attractive in make-up, and its brilliant and artistic cover will draw the children first into looking at it and then into reading it.

The above is the initial volume of the new *True Story Series of Lives of Great Men.* Other volumes in preparation.

www.ingramcontent.com/pod-product-compliance
Lightning Source LLC
Chambersburg PA
CBHW021532110726
47902CB00004B/848